PAIGE TURNER
GOES TO YELLOWSTONE

Also by Christina Hill

Paige Turner (#1)
Thirst Trapp Farms
Thirst Trapp Wedding
Tips Up
Love at First Flight
Love has a Name (#1)
To Love Again (#2)
Love Finds a Way (#3)

PAIGE TURNER
GOES TO YELLOWSTONE

CHRISTINA HILL

Copyright © 2025 by Christina Hill

All rights reserved.

No part of this publication may be reproduced, distributed, or transmitted in any form or by any means, including photocopying, recording, or other electronic or mechanical methods, without the prior written permission of the publisher, except as permitted by U.S. copyright law. For permission requests, contact [include publisher/author contact info].

The story, all names, characters, and incidents portrayed in this production are fictitious. No identification with actual persons (living or deceased), places, buildings, and products is intended or should be inferred.

Paperback ISBN: 979-8-9857199-5-6

Book Cover by Melissa Doughty.

Edited by Tracey Barski.

PAIGE'S
Roadtrip Playlist

BOULEVARD OF BROKEN DREAMS
GREEN DAY

IF I HAD EYES
JACK JOHNSON

BAD BLOOD
TAYLOR SWIFT

WHAT'S YOUR FANTASY
LUDACRIS

WE WILL ROCK YOU
QUEEN

MONTANA
OWL CITY

9 TO 5
DOLLY PARTON

To the ones wondering if they should take that trip...
Consider this your sign.

1

Paige

Today is the day I bury myself.

The *old* self that is.

I'm only being partially dramatic on this one since tomorrow, I set a metaphorical sail and journey to the great beyond.

As in the open road, not the grave...

Okay, I need to work on this a bit more.

What I'm trying to say is I'm leaving.

I'm leaving my apartment—the one in the basement of my childhood home.

I'm leaving my parents. But not until after they gave me a phone book of numbers I should call for all sorts of issues ranging from popped tires to gynecologists in other states.

I'm leaving my sister, Constance. Although she reminds me she'll still haunt my dreams every night. How sweet of her.

And I'm leaving my best friends.

This one might be the hardest. We've barely been away from each other for more than a week on family vacations or bouts of influenza or chicken pox. Come to think of it, Rhodes and I had chicken pox at the same time in seventh grade. A difficult era for all of us, including back scratches and oatmeal baths...together.

Relax. We were in swimsuits.

And our relationship is far more complicated than mostly clothed baths now.

Amber has already packed me a leopard print stationery set that will allow me to send her one letter every hour while I'm gone, and Rhodes has asked me if the water tank in Vincent VanGo, my 2000 Chevy Express camper van—a.k.a. my home on wheels for this next chunk of time—is full.

I should probably figure out what a water tank is.

Right after I add wallpaper to every interior wall.

"This print is even better in person," I say, standing outside the double doors at the side of the van to admire my—*Rhodes'*—handiwork.

He grunts as he sits back on his heels. "You don't think it'll get weird having printed eyeballs looking at you all the time?"

I quirk my head to the side and study the black eyes on the white backdrop. "They're watching over me."

"Whatever you say," he mumbles and scrapes a tool to help flatten out any air bubbles.

There's an underlying tension in his shoulders and tone I've been ignoring for the past two weeks after he told me how he felt. *He likes me.* Sure, I feel the same way about him, but it doesn't mean I'm going to stop my life for a man.

Well, not this time.

I've done it too many times in the past. But Future Me is learning from her mistakes.

Plus, Rhodes pretended to be *Roger Who Cleans*, texting me for a week straight after my coworker recommended I do a blind dating experiment with three men. He lied about who he was, and when he arrived at the reveal, I really showed him how angry I was.

By kissing him.

I might want to do it again one-hundred and two more times, but we—*I*—shouldn't.

This journey is as much about finding myself as it is time to sort through my feelings for my best friend. He's apparently liked me for a lot longer than I've realized, according to Amber. And all of these new feelings are bubbling out of me like boiling water in a pot.

I need a lid and to turn down the heat.

"Is there anything else you need?" Rhodes asks, unfolding himself from my van and standing beside me. More like *towering* over me. He's too tall, and I love it. "I'll be by tomorrow to help with putting together the storage containers for under the bed."

About that. "My dad already did it."

"Oh. Alright then. What else can I—"

"I'm leaving," I blurt out, turning to face him.

He pivots toward me, his dark, disheveled hair falling over his forehead. The T-shirt he's wearing has a hole in the neck and has been lovingly known as his *work shirt* for years, and his jeans hang low on his tapered hips. But it's his forearms I have to peel my eyes away from.

I'm going to miss those, too.

His laugh is low and clipped. "I know."

"No, like..." Why is this so hard to get out? "Like I'm leaving tomorrow...morning."

His eyes widen, and he nods his head for an incalculable amount of time. "I thought you were leaving in another week. There's still stuff to do. And the sound the van makes when you put it in reverse needs fixing."

"I know, I know." I close my eyes briefly and talk with my hands. "It sounds like a pack of crows being run over."

He lowers his brows. "I think that's called a *murder*."

"Fascinating." That makes a lot of sense. "But I'm going to head out early."

He shifts on his feet and grabs opposite elbows. "And what about the rest of the work?"

Do not look at his forearms. "I'll do them on the road."

Dad has already packed me a small tool kit with screws and things named *Phillip* and *Allen*. I'm sure I can fix the last few things. I've already packed up everything I need from my basement apartment, leaving the rest for chance with Constance.

His jaw locks, and his teeth grind together behind his cheek. "Okay."

"Okay," I confirm.

I can tell he isn't thrilled by this. Maybe it's because he was hoping for me to change my mind and confess my undying love for him. I've been close. It's not that my love for him doesn't exist, but I need to make sure it's real and not clouded by *his* feelings. And I need to do this, venture out on my own without relying on him or anyone else to tell me what my life should look like.

I'm sold out for this plan.

The one I still need to flesh out.

In the last three weeks, I've broken up with another boyfriend, quit my job working at Upstairs Closet Thrift, and kissed my best friend.

I need a minute.

He shoves his hands in his pockets and rocks on his feet. "So, this is goodbye?"

"Only for a couple of weeks. Maybe less. Maybe more." I try to comfort him, but it doesn't seem to work.

In reality, I'm comforting myself because as much as I want—*need*—to do this, I hate the idea of doing it alone. No one will be there with me, holding my hand and telling me I've got this. It's the point of this whole trip but also the cause of my watery eyes.

Rhodes looks up, clocking my tears in seconds. "Do you want a hug?"

"Yes." I fall into his chest with a thud, gripping his waist like I'm a desperate person or something. I haven't even left yet.

But somehow, this is getting real.

I moved up my timeline because I knew how hard this part was going to be, and I didn't want to prolong it. Waiting wouldn't change the fact I'm leaving. So, I surprised my other best friend, Amber, this morning when she dropped off coffee and my favorite blueberry muffin after her early morning shift at the coffee stand. And now, I'm telling Rhodes, which feels harder.

I was resolved to let my feelings go, but after waking them up from a long winter's sleep, I don't know how to do that. It's confusing and frustrating all in one awful package of stomach aches and sweaty palms.

"Don't forget about me, okay?" I breathe into his chest through my barely restrained emotions.

"You don't have to go," he says. "We could take the van on a few weekend trips; you don't have to drive to Montana."

I close my eyes, and more tears fall as I try to think of words to convince him of my decision. But the only ones that come are, "But I do."

He props his chin on the top of my head. "I know you do. It's alright."

I don't believe him, but it will have to be good enough.

We aren't leaving things on the best of terms. He wants a relationship, and I want…TBD. Until then, we're best friends who are there for each other, so I let him be here for me now.

"Cleocatra is going to miss you. A lot," I tell him, flattening my palms on his midback.

"Will you tell her I'll miss her, too?"

"Of course."

He squeezes me tighter. "Tell her I'll never forget about her."

"I'll tell her," I whisper.

He's not really talking about my precious kitty angel, Cleo. She'd hate to know she was in the middle of whatever weird thing we have going, but I know we need to get these words out somehow. Rhodes doesn't have to remind me about the kiss we shared a couple of weeks ago. I remember it in details that still make me blush.

"And tell her to ease up on the gas pedal sometimes."

I laugh into his chest, confirming my suspicions. Then by sheer force of will, I pull back and wipe my nose, keeping my gaze square to the ground. "Cleo's going to figure things out and hope that she has more answers by the time she gets back from this trip."

He doesn't move away as I admit things I haven't been able to. "There's no pressure from me. Just let Cleo know I'll always be around."

"I will," I say, lifting my eyes to his.

They're watery, like mine, but neither of us lets them fall.

I don't know the kind of person I'll be when I return. If I'll want the same things I did before, or if I'll suddenly enjoy eating portobello mushrooms as much as I love buying cutesy items shaped like them. There's an unknown waiting period ahead, but as hard as this is, I'm confident in my decision.

He swipes his thumb under my lashes, catching a tear I thought I kept in. "I love you, Paige."

My lips part, and I start blinking rapidly to quell more tears from spilling.

He drops his hand and rushes to add, "I don't expect you to say it back. In fact, I don't want you to unless you really mean it. Not in a friendly way, at least. And when you figure out how you feel about me, I promise I'll accept it." Pausing, he breathes a sigh. "Can we still text?"

Words are hard, so I nod.

He nods, too, then tucks his hands in his pockets and walks backward toward the curb where his tiny car is parked. Minuscule might be the better word since his head threatens to puncture a hole in the roof. But I still love this about him. His understated confidence in just about everything, the steady way he enters situations like a natural, and how he doesn't question what his heart is telling him.

I wish mine would do the same.

Instead, she's a filthy liar who has liked anything with a pulse.

He starts the engine and waves before pulling away from the curb and buzzing away like a little bumble bee determined to find the next flower.

I finally let the breath rattling in my chest out with a shaky exhale. "Goodbye, Rhodes."

The tears are back and falling with a force that has me covering my mouth to hide the gasps. It hurts more than I expected.

I may not know what I want in life, but it's official, I hate goodbyes.

2

RHODES

I drive away from the scene of the crime in shock.

But I still manage to turn on an emo playlist almost entirely made up of Green Day songs and start screaming the lyrics at the top of my lungs to cope with this goodbye.

I *hate* it.

Saying goodbye to the woman I love, who I think shares my feelings, and hoping she returns in a few weeks, maybe more or less, is…unsettling. What if she decides to stay in Montana or Wyoming? What if she wants to continue traveling? What if she finds a hot cowboy and doesn't need me anymore? There are so many possibilities, and I don't want to think about any of them. But that's also impossible since losing her has been top of mind for the two weeks since we kissed, she pulled back, and then doubled down by purchasing a camper.

I turn up the music even louder and pound the hammering beat into my steering wheel. There are tears in my eyes that blur my vision and force my vocal cords to vibrate and twitch with emotions I have no control over.

She's leaving me.

And I may never get her back.

She's never done this before—moved to other parts of the country that required a phone call or text to keep in touch. But this is still different because I told her I *love* her. It feels more like a rejection even if this trip is designed to help Paige find herself, which is exactly what she should do. It's important and necessary and right.

It's what I've wanted for her. I knew she wasn't ready for a committed relationship. Besides the revolving door of boyfriends in her life, I knew there was more she needed to figure out. She wants to know how to stand on her own two feet. It doesn't matter that I can see the feet she's standing on, and the resolve she already possesses to discover what she really wants. She has to realize it herself.

But it still hurts.

I'm crushed, squashed like a poor bug on a windshield that was probably just minding its business, flying around, loving people, until *WHAM*! Dead.

How am I supposed to protect her when she's gone?

I'm completely powerless.

My love is like a balloon floating without a string, a left shoe without the right one, and lots of other depressing analogies that have me completely reeling.

Paige leaving might just be my kryptonite because I feel as though I'm coming apart from the inside out. I have no control in this situation, and I don't like it. This whole scenario reminds me of what it felt like with my dad's health struggles.

No control.

It's probably why I avoided telling Paige how I felt because these emotions are all too big, too wild for my liking. It was easier to hide them. They wouldn't be as real that way. But here I am, living with my heart outside my fucking body.

When I swerve outside the lane toward the shoulder, I determine I'm in no shape to drive right now. I need to calm down, get my emotions locked in handcuffs.

Almost to Ruston Way, a stretch of road bordering the water along Puget Sound, I look for the nearest parking lot, pull in, and wrestle with my seatbelt before getting out of the car. It's closest to the train tracks, which sit higher on the bluff than the gravel rocks I'm pacing on. They crunch under my feet and have somehow become the loudest noise despite leaving my car door open and the music blaring.

My hands are in my hair, and I tug. Hard. Trying to feel something other than the noise my heart makes as it breaks.

I'm losing her.

And I have to figure out how to be okay with that.

This is her journey and not mine.

There's a part of me that holds this guilt for not telling her how I feel sooner and waiting until we were doing some ridiculous blind dating experiment to do so. The nights I've laid in bed thinking about the last couple of weeks and how much it's changed us makes me want to invent a time machine and go back to how things were when we were just friends.

But I can't do that.

Instead, I've paused my entire life to spend that time regretting the lie I told.

I even posted an old stop-motion video last week since I didn't have the energy—or time outside of berating myself—to film, edit, and post a new one. I've *never* had to do that. I've always been able to get my work done when I needed to. I love what I do. But not this time. Not now.

It was easier when we were friends, and the most I had to worry about was whether she wanted me to bring Chinese or Thai food over to her house while we watched *Love is Blind*, and which boyfriend's name I needed to forget. Now I'm not so sure we can ever go back to that, or even close to it.

I pound at my chest, willing the traitorous organ inside to sit back down and shut the hell up. My confession did something to me. It opened me up to possibilities and hope and a whole lot of hormones I've been shoving down, down, down. But it won't listen. It's worse, and now I'm forced to just be okay with the complete havoc it's having in my life.

It's hard *not* to think my love drove her away.

She's leaving isn't she?

I'm split in two, wanting her to have everything she needs and wants in life while also feeling completely helpless. This much chaos in my life is making me sick.

I drop my hands to my side and stare up at the gray sky, which is more of a constant in Washington than any other color. To some, it's dreary. But I love it. There's a comfort in the particular dark, moody shade today and how it mimics the overturned tables inside me.

This isn't going to be easy—the letting go, the loss of control, the questioning. But I have to. For Paige's sake, I need to. For a potential future with her, I will. I remind myself I don't have to like it, I don't have to agree, but I have to accept it.

In the meantime, I'll just need to be okay.

She said we can still keep in touch. I can text her without having to hide behind *Roger Who Cleans* anymore. I'll throw myself into work and keep busy while she's gone and force Amber to hang out with me every once in a while, which does seem odd now that we aren't a trio.

It's fine. I'm fine. This will all be *fine*.

I exhale deeply, puffing out my cheeks and resting firm hands on the hood of my car to steady my swaying body. I've been wanting to spend more time at the gym anyway. I can meal prep for the entire month, or join a bowling league if I want.

Maybe this won't be so bad, enjoyable even.

"Shit," I say on another exhale.

This is going to suck.

3

Paige

I didn't sleep at all last night.

I'd like to blame it on the fact Cleo was jumping on my feet under the covers anytime I moved them, but she always does that. It could have been the faint noises traveling through the return vents from Constance's room. She was up late playing some kind of game that required a lot of groaning and smack talk.

But I'm fairly used to her night owl ways, too.

No. I'm pretty sure I didn't sleep because I'm having second thoughts.

Maybe Rhodes has a point, and instead of traveling across multiple states alone, I should just take a few shorter trips. All night I kept thinking about everything that could go wrong: flat tires, kidnappers, road pirates, bad weather, bears, etc. The list I made in my head last night while I should have been sleeping is longer than Santa's Naughty *and* Nice list.

I tap my phone screen beside my bed to check the time yet again and decide five a.m. is a perfectly reasonable time for someone to get up.

Someone who has a death wish, sure, but acceptable.

I throw the covers back, missing Cleo's sprawled body by an inch, and slip my feet into the banana slippers Amber got me for my birthday last year. This year, we won't be together, though. I'll be on the open road. Alone.

Stop it!

I'm doing this for a reason.

I'm going to morph into an independent badass by the end of this trip.

Shaking my head, I shuffle my feet to the bathroom, which is basically a small closet behind my "kitchen," a counter with a hot plate for a stove and a mini fridge below it. I brush through my shoulder length red hair that is every bit as frightful as the mirror says it is, scrub my teeth, and wash my face, packing my supplies into a small toiletries bag I'll be taking with me. I top off the look with my circular, dark-rimmed glasses that hide the fear in my eyes.

I get a strong urge to pack the bag into the van right away so I don't forget it, so without changing into shoes, I unlock the twenty-five deadbolts I—*Rhodes*—put on the door to my basement apartment when I first moved in and head for the van. Unsurprisingly, it's still where I left it, parked in the center of the driveway in order to have enough space to pack and finish the odd jobs. Dad helped me load the remaining storage bins under the bed last night and stocked the pantry with food items.

I'm sure my parents will be excited to have this monstrosity out of their driveway again, but it only makes my anxiety spike to an uncomfortable level.

They aren't coming with me.

A part of me, while small, is looking forward to this. It's easier to be dependent on people when they are right there, in your space, your life. But when they aren't, they are less of a crutch. I think that's what has happened to me. I rely on them too much.

Like last month when I was short on rent, and my parents reminded me I don't pay anything to live here. Or recently when I took Mom to my dental appointment, and the hygienist asked if she'd be staying, to which we both looked at her with a *duh* expression. Not to mention Dad's way of picking up nearly two of everything from the grocery store, including my favorite kind of chocolate, to make sure I have a stocked pantry.

This needs to stop.

I'm almost thirty!

I love my family, but without them, I fear I might literally starve to death. But how else am I supposed to learn?

I take a deep breath and open one of the two side doors that sound like two squirrels fighting to put my mind at ease that everything is the exact same as it was yesterday. The wallpaper is still where it should be, the pots and pans are still in the single basin sink that is smaller than a toilet bowl, and my accent pillows are thrown in a heap on the full-size bed at the back.

The tension in my shoulders starts to recede, and a hint of a smile tugs at the corner of my lips. Worry and fear, and stress leaves my body when I think about my adventure. The solo traveler making it happen on the open road. It'll be worth every penny I've scrounged up to have an experience like this one. It has to because I don't want my thirties to be like my twenties: aimless.

"Today's the day," I hear someone say behind me.

I have a guess at who it is. Pivoting quickly, I wave to Machete Lady, who is sharpening her swords on a rock. "Good morning. We ride at dawn."

She looks off toward the sun peaking over the horizon. "It is dawn."

I twist my lips and decide not to explain the reference. "After dawn, then. Later. I still have a few things to pack."

She kneels to set one machete down and pick up the other. "Did you bring the knife I gave you?"

The pocket knife with twenty-four different utility uses I could never come up with—except for the scissors, which I've already used to clip a stray thread on my sweater—is tucked under my front seat.

"I sure did," I confirm.

"Good," she says with a nod. "Are you sure you don't need a machete?"

I nod emphatically. "Positive."

If I need a machete at any point in this trip then I've done it wrong.

Fiddling with the zipper on the toiletries bag, I let my doubts show. "Do you think I should do this? Go on this big road trip by myself, that is?"

What I don't ask is: *should I also rethink the machete?*

She braces her hands on her legs when she stands and tosses her long, black braid over her shoulder. "Depends."

Great. I knew I bit off more than I should.

"Why are you going?" Her stare is level and steady.

I squirm a little and try to remember *why*. If I hadn't been asking myself this question for the last couple of weeks, I wouldn't be prepared to answer. But it's been the only thing I've been able to come back to any time I've tried talking myself out of going.

"I've never really taken the time to think about what I wanted or taken a risk like this on my own. My parents and friends have always been there, encouraging me toward particular avenues and possibilities, picking me back up when my ideas fail." I pause, restraining the emotions clawing up my throat. "I want to do this on my own and figure out what I want my life to look like at the end."

The knife she gave me has more pockets than the cargo pants she wipes her hands on. "And you have to do it alone?"

I shift on my feet. "I mean, yeah. I've always had their input and support. I want to do this on my own."

Why does it feel like I'm trying to convince her?

Probably because I'm still trying to convince myself.

She nods slowly, methodically, as if the silence between our words isn't currently being devoured by all of the chirping birds. "I hope you figure out what you want."

My smile is pinched, if only because it feels like maybe she isn't saying something more. We aren't super close like she and Constance apparently are, but she seems to be there whenever I need someone to talk to.

"Why does it sound like you don't agree?" I ask in a brazen attempt to get the answers I need or want.

"I think you're going to find something out there on the road." She brackets her hips with her hands. "But road trips have a way of showing us what we didn't expect instead of what we did. They might seem linear—going from point A to point B—but they aren't."

There are so many layers to her response I don't know how to decipher all of them. I open my mouth to say something, but Constance steals my next words.

"Decided to slash your own tires to put yourself out of the misery that is this trip?"

I turn around and shift in time to see Constance slowly walking down the front steps. Her hands are at her sides, and are those…machetes?

"What the hell—"

"Pearl," Constance says with a nod toward our neighbor.

"Constance."

"Why are you holding those—"

"Don't ask questions," Constance cuts me off. "Are you leaving?"

The irony of her asking me a question isn't lost, but I simply smile and clutch my toiletries bag closer to my chest for protection. I'm surrounded by knives. "Not yet."

"A shame."

I laugh even though it's clipped. A surge of affection and warmth passes over me, and I'm all too aware of how much I'm going to miss my sister. Sure, she has machetes in her hands, but I don't let it stop me from wrapping her in a tight hug when she gets close enough.

"I'm going to miss you," I tell her.

She doesn't move, but I think that's because her arms are pinned to her sides, and she doesn't have that option.

"Don't change while I'm gone."

Her breathing is strained. "Don't...plan...on it."

I let her go and take a deep breath before letting it all the way out as a car pulls up along the curb.

Rhodes.

I didn't think he would come since we said our goodbyes yesterday. Suddenly, my hands are sweaty, and my stomach feels as though it will fall out of my ass.

Make that two cars since Amber is pulling up behind him and crawling out of hers.

They aren't supposed to be here. One goodbye yesterday was good enough.

"You're up early," I yell at both of them.

Amber wraps her beige sweater around her tighter as she approaches. "It's your fault. You're leaving us."

Touché.

Rhodes puts his hands in his pockets and sidles up beside Amber. "All packed?"

I peer at the toiletries bag I'm holding. "Not exactly. You didn't have to come, you know."

"We did." His stare is unwavering. "Figured you'd be up early."

Tears rush to my eyes because I'm such a sentimental mess. My best friends know me so well, the parts of me that wake up in a torment of anxious thoughts and a lack of focus because I've decided to take a last-minute self-discovery journey. Not that this has ever happened before, but it's nice to know I don't have to try and explain what's going on in my head.

It's an absolute nightmare in there right now.

Amber extends her hand with a coffee I hadn't noticed at first.

I want to cry and thank her, but with Constance and Machete Lady comparing swords behind us, I try to keep it light by tugging her into a hug and whispering how much I love her instead.

There might also be tears that slip out.

Mom chooses this moment to pop her head out the front door. "Who wants breakfast? I made a thousand waffles and every egg I have in this house." She shuts the door without waiting for our answer.

Clearly, this is an act of stress cooking.

I pull away from Amber and greedily take the offered coffee to guzzle a sip, burning my tongue in the process. I wince. "I'm going to remember this moment all week now that I've singed my taste buds."

"My plan exactly," Amber says with a smile.

I bounce my gaze to Rhodes, who is being quiet. *Too* quiet.

He clears his throat, pulls a journal from behind his back, and holds it out to me. "This is for you to write about your trip."

I take the small, tan leather-bound notebook from him, turning it over in my hand only to notice my name etched into the side. "My very own *Little House on the Prairie* journal!"

He beams with a smile. "You can write about anything you want, but don't forget to include all the boring stuff, too."

There's a catch in my throat as I drag my thumb across the soft leather. The weird part about going on a trip like this is I have no clue what's going in this journal yet. I don't know what the boring moments will look like or the epic ones I hope to have. The unknown of it feels like the actual adventure.

"Thank you," I say quietly, then look up at him.

He's staring directly into the deeper layers of me, just like I knew he would be. It's how he always looks at me. It wasn't until recently I figured out it was because he liked me. Do I look at him like this? Eyes slightly lowered but still ready to catch mine at every glance?

Someone clangs two machetes together, startling me out of my thoughts. It's an abrasive sound that grates on my remaining sanity but also snaps me back into the present moment.

I shake my head and reach to give Rhodes a quick hug. It isn't the kind I would've given him minutes ago, but it's the kind I need to offer him. My heart and mind have been in a heated war about how to act around him these last couple of weeks, and I've somehow managed not to blur any lines. I just have to make it through a little while longer.

"Can we help load anything before we eat those waffles?" Rhodes asks, hands back in the protection of his pockets.

I laugh and wave for them to follow me toward my apartment door, saying over my shoulder, "Do you think my sewing machine will fit?"

Rhodes and Amber both speak at the same time. "No!"

I love them, but I'm still going to try.

4

RHODES

I'm pathetic.

Paige only left this morning, and I'm already at a loss for what to do with myself.

I worked out for a bit before I got distracted thinking about Paige and almost dropped a weight on my foot, missed a call from Mom after I told her to reach out at that time, and forgot my keys on the rung of my locker, forcing me to walk all the way back to get them in order to get into my apartment. I also haven't made it to the grocery store in a few days, so it looks like I'm going to go hungry this week.

Flat on my back, I'm staring at the ceiling and thinking about the good old days when I'd be picking up Paige from Upstairs Closet Thrift in an hour, hearing about her day, and offering her an apple or granola bar since she likely forgot to eat lunch.

She's probably well into her journey, playing music that's too loud to hear anything else, and eating Gushers. I can say this for certain since I saw them on the front seat before she left, and I helped curate her playlist.

There's no way I'm going to be able to handle this for the next few weeks or however long it will take. That might be the worst part—a vague understanding of time. If I knew it was only a week or two, I might be able to manage. But, just like with Dad's recovery, I don't know how long I'm in this for. I don't like the instability of it all.

Maybe it wouldn't be so bad if I hadn't said *I love you*?

Or maybe there's just no hope for me.

I'm gone for this woman. Always have been.

I sit up and start to pace my living room. There's got to be something else I can do that will keep me from following her in my car.

I pick up my phone and stare at my last texts to Paige:

> Me:
> I slipped a gas card in the cupholder. Don't forget to use it!

> Me:
> Have a great time.

> Me:
> I miss you already.

Yeah. There's probably a really good reason why Paige feels like she needs to take this solo trip, and it likely has to do with the fact we're always around each other. How else is she supposed to figure out what she really wants and whether that includes me when I'm breathing down her neck? I'm channeling a lost dog on the streets right now without my best friend. What does that say about me?

That I need a hobby. ASAP.

I scroll down to Amber's contact and click on it, tapping my fingers on the window sill in time with every ring.

"Are you bored yet?" Amber asks when she answers on the fifth ring.

"I'm...contemplating."

She sighs. "You have to let her go, Rhodes."

"I did!" I protest. "We both watched her drive off, didn't we? After hitting the mailbox and causing Machete Lady to spear the Rhododendron, but she's gone, Amber, and I didn't chase after her."

But I wanted to.

"Yes, but how many times have you almost decided to get in your wee little car and follow her down I-90?"

More than half a dozen in the last hour, at least.

"Enough to know I need a hobby," I state, tracing the window lock. I sigh heavily. "I need something to take my mind off Paige."

"Scrapbooking?"

"Is that still a thing?"

The milk frother picks up in the background. "It was a hot hobby there for a while. You could likely find all of the supplies at Upstairs Closet."

"Pass."

"How about video games?"

I've never been good at sitting for long periods of time. "That sounds like mental and physical suffering I don't want. It needs to be active. Preferably something that involves hitting, punching, or throwing."

"Have you ever tried pickleball?" she asks. "It's basically all three of those things."

"Punching?"

She scoffs. "Only if you lose."

I've never been a big sports guy. I played soccer when I was younger and warmed the bench for the other basketball players in middle school before deciding cameras were a lot more interesting to me.

"Is pickleball the one with the table?" I ask, leaning against the wall.

"That's ping pong. Or maybe it's called table tennis?" Something drops on her end until I realize it was her phone since it sounds like she fumbles around for it. "Sorry. I'm at work and need to put you on speakerphone while I make this iced latte."

Now I'm thirsty.

"Don't be fooled, Rhodes. Pickleball has gained more popularity in recent years, and it's an Olympic sport."

I laugh. "So is break dancing, apparently. That doesn't mean a whole lot, Amber. I just need to know if it will take my mind off Paige."

The espresso grinder roars to life on her end, and when it stops, I know she's tamping down the shots. I've seen the process enough times since Paige would normally ask me to swing by the stand before or after work, usually both.

Damn it. *Paige*.

I really can't stop thinking about her.

I shake my head, pushing off the wall to shuffle through my dresser drawer for shorts. "Teach me how to play pickleball today after work."

She laughs as a straw squeaks being shoved into the cup. "Just because I know what pickleball is—thank you for coming!—doesn't mean I know how to play."

"We'll figure it out together then. I'm sure my gym has what we need, but I'll call to confirm and let you know."

"Rhodes, I fully support you wanting to do something productive to keep you from going insane over Paige leaving and not returning your feelings—"

"To be determined, Amber! She never said she didn't like me. AND she kissed me back." It was the best kiss of my life, in fact.

"Yes, she kissed you. But she's also confused right now, hence the birthday crises she's experiencing."

I shove my drawer closed when I get what I need. "You think she's doing this because she's about to turn thirty?"

When I turned thirty, I went to an Italian restaurant with Amber and Paige and was home and in bed by 8:30 p.m. No big revelations and definitely no fleeing the state.

But I'd already been well into my "career" at this point, making stop-motion video clips that not only made people smile from worlds away but also paid the bills. I know Paige feels like she's never had a serious grown-up job before, and that makes her feel aimless, but what even is that? Do I have a grown-up job? Is it something corporate with suits and ties, slacks and pumps? I don't think so…

"Maybe. Probably," Amber says, though her voice sounds as if she's in the stock room grabbing more supplies. "But while she's on her journey, you need to go on yours. Preferably alone. As in, without *me*."

"Six o'clock. My gym unless I text you otherwise." My words are stern and commanding, which leaves me little hope she's going to agree.

"Rhodes," she whines.

"Please, Amber. I need this. I need to forget. I'm calling in my friend card."

She laughs. "You mean the slips of paper we wrote on and gave to each other in case something ever came up where we needed the others to step in?"

"Yes, that one," I confirm, tossing a shirt on the bed.

"You still have yours? We were like ten."

"Thirteen, actually, and I don't know where the card is, but I never used mine. You and Paige had already handed yours over by the end of the day."

There's a deep sigh on her end while I hold my breath.

"Make it 6:30. I need to go home and grab my clothes for sweating."

"IT'S THE POLO shirt, I swear. It's a curse." Amber huffs, bracing her hands on her knees. "When did you even buy that?"

I pluck at the collar of my shirt, which also happens to be plastered to my body like a second skin from sweat. "I honestly can't remember."

My gym, located below my apartment, had all the necessary gear for pickleball. Amber was right. It really is an up-and-coming sport. They also had two rowdy players—Jim and Agnes—eager to play us. At first, I didn't think it would be an issue to pair up since they looked as if they had AARP memberships and maybe a cup beside their beds for dentures.

Is that even a thing? Seems unhygienic.

Turns out they're retired, which isn't all that surprising. What is a shocker is how well they play. All the extra time has given them more opportunity to practice.

Amber falls to her knees on the court. "I need…water…stat."

I smile at Jim and Agnes, signaling a time-out so I can get my partner more water. She's already finished off her bottle and is halfway through mine. We're both going to need plenty of electrolytes after this game. Jim and Agnes have a mean backhand while we've spent most of the time running after the ball rather than hitting it.

Unscrewing the cap, I chug some water and then offer it to Amber, who is now flat on her back. She opens her mouth. "Just pour it in."

"I'm going to spill it all over you and the court if I do that," I say, sticking out my hand. "Let me help you up. We can take five on the bench."

"Can't. Move."

I roll my eyes and cap the water bottle again so I can peel my teammate off the floor. She groans when I lift under her arms and force her to her feet.

"Are my legs still attached?" she asks, peering down, even though she's slowly shuffling toward the bench seat.

"Yes," I confirm while massaging my upper thighs. I wildly underestimated the physical output this sport would require of us.

Amber sits on the bench and leans against the wall, sticking out her hand for the water bottle. I oblige and hand it over. "They're trying to kill us, I think," Amber says, dark hair plastered to the sides of her face.

I look over my shoulder. Jim is holding Agnes' hand so she can balance on one leg while stretching her quad. "God, they're like...bionic."

"You're right about that." Amber gulps the rest of the water. "Agnes had her hip replaced and both knees within the last five years."

"How do you know?" I ask, brows furrowed.

"Before the game in the bathroom. She seemed so sweet back then."

"Well, good news..." I open my palms in a wide gesture. "I haven't thought about Paige in the last thirty minutes we've been playing!"

Amber goes still. "We've only been playing for thirty minutes?"

I check the clock. "Sorry. Thirty-five minutes."

She groans and sinks further into the wall, widening her knees. "How are you not dying right now?"

"I eat well and work out every day?"

"I hate you."

"You can come to the gym with me this week, hit the weights before we take on Jim and Agnes again—"

"Again?!" Amber yells, and I have to smile at the elderly couple over my shoulder so they know we're good. Well, mostly.

"Didn't you hear the part about how I haven't been thinking about Paige?"

"You are now!"

I glare at her. "Because we've stopped playing. Come on, Amber. This is good for me. It's helping. And after the shit couple weeks I've had, I feel *unstoppable*."

Mentally, I haven't been in the best place. I know I haven't been dealing with the rejection or the lack of control well. I held everything I'd ever wanted for a few short seconds before she shoved me into limbo. It was a huge hit, plus it's cold and dark and lonely here. And there is only so much cleaning one person can take under this kind of stress. I'm positive I've reached that limit.

I even tried making candles like Paige always does when she's in a slump. Now my kitchen rug has melted wax all over it, and I've got a burn shaped like Mickey Mouse on my forearm.

"Please, Amber. I just need to play for the next however long Paige is gone, and then when she's back, I'll know if I need to join a league or not."

Her eyes snap to mine. "You can't be serious."

Oh, but I am.

If Paige wants nothing more to do with me, I'll likely need to start preparing for the Olympics.

My expression softens, but I don't break eye contact.

"Oh shit. You are," she whispers.

"Please?"

She huffs. "Fine. But you owe me a weekly massage at the fancy spa here."

"I'll make your first appointment when we leave."

Her gaze tracks to Jim and Agnes, jogging in place. "Okay then. Help me up. I think my feet have been chopped off."

5

Paige

I forgot how fun driving is.

It's been a while since I've sat behind a wheel. Rhodes, or one of my family members, has been driving me everywhere since the wreck that shall not be remembered.

I lost a headlight and a good deal of my front bumper, though. Repairs that made it worth saving up for a new vehicle. Even if said *new* vehicle is actually a very old one with a few rips in the upholstery and has a bed and sink in the back.

But this is nice.

Three hours into my drive, and "If I Had Eyes" by Jack Johnson blares through the speakers while I sing every lyric, and Cleo sits in her specially designed catseat. Really, it's just a cat bed with a small leash that attaches to her harness and the headrest in the passenger bucket seat that swivels forward and back. Safety first. She seems to be enjoying the sunbeams bursting through the side windows while we traverse through a winding stretch of concrete and tan rolling hills in every other direction.

It's perfect.

So perfect that I forget I'm on cruise control when it happens.

I forget a lot of things.

Like how thankful I am for Cleo's catseat.

Or how I'm at least a half-mile behind the car in front of me.

I definitely forget which pedal is the gas and which is the brake.

Not until after I scream and grip the steering wheel with the force of an iron clamp while my life flashes before my eyes when a bird swoops too close, too low, too late.

Cleo doesn't make a sound while my horror movie screams fill the entire van. I'm sure my high pitch isn't helping keep her calm. It isn't helping me, either.

I finally slam on the brakes and swerve, hoping to avoid getting rear-ended. The only benefit to driving this stretch of Washington is that there are more wind turbines than vehicles. No one is behind me when I check my mirrors.

My breathing is ragged and uneven as I clutch my chest, firmly parked in the middle of the lane, trying to make sense of what just happened.

I'm alive.

Cleo's alive.

Vincent VanGo is alive.

The bird that flew in front of me…TBD.

With a shaky hand, I turn down Jack, who is in the middle of singing one of my favorite lines about people being together but lonely.

There's no time for introspection now, Jack!

"Oh, God. Oh, God." I slowly navigate to the side of the road with jittery hands and flashbacks from my last accident. "Oh. My. God."

I close my eyes and open them again. Still here. Which means the bird is probably…not. But I can't just leave it. The bird…its family…other cars could—

A car whooshes past, rattling my vehicle with the wind impact.

"I have to go back," I say to myself. "The bird. It needs my help."

I throw Vincent in reverse, the awful sound still loudly–and proudly–screeching like a pair of mating coyotes.

Cleo meows from her throne, doing her best to warn me, but I'm already unlocking my door and peering behind me for any traffic. There are no cars, so I get out and slam the door behind me, looking a few paces back for the slaughterhouse I just erected in the middle of the highway.

But that's not what I see.

"It's—" I don't have time to finish my sentence when a wing flaps and is raised perpendicular to the road.

I start jogging back, holding my glasses so they don't fly off my face and retracing the skid marks I created when I hit the brakes.

The bird is... "Alive!" I scream out loud.

A smile splits my face until I realize, yes, it's alive, but I'm in the middle of nowhere. What am I supposed to do? Its other wing looks badly injured from my place on the side of the road, but I don't know the extent of its injuries until I get closer.

I have to get closer.

Looking both ways again, I confirm I'm in the clear and tentatively walk closer. The bird isn't making a sound apart from its wing flapping. That isn't good.

"Hey, birdie..."

The image I'm met with is one I'll never be able to unsee.

I rear back, covering my mouth and looking anywhere but the ground. It's not dead, but it's struggling. There is red and feathers, and possibly a spleen on the cement that certainly belongs inside the bird's body.

"Paige, you have to do something!" I practically yell at myself. "You can't leave this poor bird here to die. You did this! Fix it."

I glance around me again just as another car on the opposite side of the road passes by with a velocity that flips my hair into my face. I brush the shoulder-length strands away from my mouth and yank my phone from my pocket as I walk toward the side of the road again.

I've never done this before. Been this person who hits an animal only to leave them helpless. Probably because I've never hit anything. I'm shaking violently while I cradle my head in my hands, thinking of what the hell I'm supposed to do about this.

Mom will know.

But she doesn't answer. Not uncommon during the middle of the day since she works as a financial advisor in the area and often works weekends, so I dial Dad.

No answer.

Don't they know I'm out on the open road right now, and anything could happen?

Yeah, like you mutilating a poor, helpless bird.

It begins to squawk, but it sounds strangled and hoarse, like its vocal cords were injured in the accident, too.

"I know; I'm trying to help you. Hold on!"

Another car approaches, so I step back in case I'm not visible—*impossible*—and start wildly waving my arms and jabbing my fingers at the bird in order to warn them not to hit it. That's the last thing I need to witness.

Instead, I seem to have alerted them that I'm in trouble since they pull to the shoulder as well.

There's a woman and man through the windshield, but they're far enough back I can't tell if they're friendly or murderers. Maybe the third option of friendly murderers.

I'll call Amber. She'll know what to do about the bird and the friendly murderers.

But she doesn't answer either.

Hours into this journey, and I already need someone. I cradle my forehead again, wiping away beads of sweat and regret. I'm going to have to call Rhodes. This was supposed to be my break-out act, where I got to figure things out on my own. Where I become a self-sufficient human who knows what to do in the face of trouble and who doesn't solve every life problem with a new boyfriend, but I can't even handle this.

"Yoo-hoo!" a voice calls.

I snap my attention back to a woman who looks to be in her mid-sixties, complete with a silk scarf around her head like she's driving a convertible and not a Mini Cooper. Her small car reminds me of—

"Answer the phone, Rhodes!" I say out loud, cradling the phone to my ear.

The woman looks kind, but that could all be a ruse. My phone just keeps ringing as she gets closer.

I peer at the bird, still flapping around in complete distress.

Answer. Answer. Answer.

He doesn't answer.

"Miss?" the woman asks hesitantly. "Are you alright?"

I end the call just as Rhodes' voicemail recording ends with a beep. "I'm..."

Alone.

I swallow and address the woman. Her smile sure is convincing enough. I mean, who stops for a stranger waving their hands around, looking like they're ready to throw rocks at their vehicle? It's probably safe to drop the murderer part of this equation.

"H-Hi, I'm Paige." I point to the road again. "There's a bird—"

"Oh my good golly gosh!" The woman squeaks like the bird is trying to. "What happened to this sweet soul?"

I immediately pick up on her Southern accent. It makes me want to curl up in her lap while she pats my back and calls me *honey*.

"I...hit...it." The words are hard to admit, but I don't have time for pride when there's a life at stake. "With my van."

I mime the blunt force impact of my front bumper and the bird with added explosive noises for effect. My swallow is hard, and I have to wipe my brow again, either from the heat of this late evening sun or my stress.

It's definitely both.

She stares blankly, then removes her sunglasses. "Well, seems like this is your first."

"My first?"

She nods with understanding and crosses her arms in front of her at the wrists. "Your first roadkill."

I look back at the bird. "I...this...we have to help it!" I start talking fast. "Do you know any vets around here? It looks like there was a lot of...trauma. I have a couple of towels to wrap it up. Maybe you or your husband can pick it up and put it in my van?"

There's no way I want to touch it.

She simply places a gentle hand on my arm. "Honey, it's time this bird meets Jesus. That's all there is to say about it."

My mouth gapes. "What? No, I'm positive we can save—"

"What seems to be the problem, Winnie?" the husband asks as he approaches.

He's wearing a plaid, short-sleeve button-up with tan cargo shorts and boat shoes, wholly out of place for the agricultural area we're in, but surprisingly very stylish for a man his age.

"She ran over a bird." She adjusts her scarf and addresses me. "This is Archie."

"What?"

"A bird," Winnie says. "She ran over a—"

"What did you say?" It takes him minutes to close the distance between their car

and where we're standing.

"The bird!" She points to the middle of the road.

"What?" he asks again.

Winnie looks like she wants to throw something at him. "Oh, for the love—"

Before she can finish, a large semi-truck barrels by us at a speed that could kill. Thankfully, we're all on the side of the road. Except…

I cover my mouth with both hands.

Winnie points at where the bird was once flapping its wing while we all stare in disbelief and horror.

Lots of horror.

She's the first to speak. "That takes care of that."

I drop my hands, staring at the nearly flattened animal I half-killed.

Archie, still unaware of everything that's happened, simply says, "What?"

Winnie and I both turn blank stares on him.

My phone screen still only touts the time and date, which are now burned into my memory forever, with a photo in the background of me sandwiched between Amber and Rhodes.

And still no missed calls or texts.

This was quite possibly the worst moment of my life, and no one was there except for two people whose first names I've only just learned.

It feels wrong in many ways.

Tears push at the backs of my eyes, a sudden urge to cry the biggest, ugliest tears I've ever experienced because I realize I'm the killer.

Winnie clears her throat. "Darling."

My eyes are glazed over, seeing her, but not really. "Yeah?"

"We all have our firsts. I'm going to do what my mama did for me once. It'll help to think of when you go to bed tonight."

I nod, agreeing to whatever comes next.

Maybe I should have asked a question.

Or two.

"WE ARE GATHERED here today to remember this sweet soul," Winnie begins, Bible open and perched on a nearby fence post. "A life that was cut too short."

I nod in agreement, holding fast to Cleo's leash so she doesn't dart out into traffic and become the next victim of mile marker 104. Winnie, Archie, Cleo, and I are all circling a mound of dirt where Russel Crow is buried twelve inches under. Roughly, of course, because I didn't have anything to measure with, and I used a cup to dig the hole.

"Let's all hold hands," Winnie says, holding hers out.

I slip the loop of Cleo's leash around my wrist and grab both of their cool, wrinkled hands in mine.

She continues. "We release this life to your eternal care forever and ever. Amen."

Winnie is still looking skyward, so I follow suit and look up, too.

Cleo tugs at the leash. There's no way Archie doesn't feel the jerk of my arm, but when I crack an eye open to check, his head is bowed in reverence. He's so still and peaceful, he truly doesn't seem bothered.

Or awake.

I quickly close my eyes and bow my head like him, hoping it'll affect me in the same way. There is clearly a moment happening, and I already feel guilty enough for killing the poor bird, I don't want to mess this up either.

Cleo doesn't stop.

She yanks and pulls until, finally, I can't take it. I open my eyes and locate her speckled body on the end of the leash.

I wish I hadn't.

One of Russel Crow's feathered wings juts up from the dirt, thanks to Cleo, who is trying to unearth the body. Her once-white paws are now covered in dirt, and is that blood?

My head whips side-to-side to see if Winnie and Archie have noticed, but their eyes are still closed. Winnie starts to sing Amazing Grace, and I take the opportunity to loop my leg around Cleo's leash to pull her back.

She's too fast and darts under my leg before I can shorten her lead.

I jerk my hand. Archie doesn't move, and Winnie starts up verse two in a louder falsetto.

I try kicking dirt at Cleo, but she's locked in. Bird is her favorite meal, and I've basically done all of the hard work for her.

With one final tug, I yank her leash back. Hard.

Unfortunately, this rattles Archie from his comatose state, and his head jerks up.

He was definitely sleeping.

Winnie opens her eyes and sees what Cleo is doing. Instead of gasping or screaming like I expect her to, she starts laughing. So hard, she's bent at the waist while I frantically pull Cleo away from her twice-murdered feast.

"What are you laughing about?" Archie asks, peering around.

I scoop up Cleo, but she jumps out of my arms to make the five-foot drop. It only makes Winnie laugh harder and Archie scratch his head more.

I'm laughing now, too, which isn't helping as I step backward, dragging Cleo like a ragdoll as I go.

Winnie wipes the tears in her eyes and looks at me with big brown eyes when I finally get my cat *mostly* under control. "Let's go get some lunch."

6

CLEOCATRA

How dare she deny me of my feast.

It's not as if she was going to eat it. My human and the other peasants covered my dinner in dirt, thinking I wouldn't want it.

They were wrong.

I was just getting started.

How rude.

I feel a strong need to pee on something now.

7

Rhodes

After scheduling a massage for Amber, I took the elevator back up to my apartment to shower and change, which is one benefit of having a full-size gym just downstairs. I might have to trade out thicker walls between my neighbors, but it's worth it.

My place is quiet.

Too quiet.

Which is weird because...thin walls. I can normally hear everything, especially those I don't want to.

The silence is starting to grate on me, so I turn on the small radio I keep in my room, an ancient device I haven't really gotten out of the habit of switching on occasionally. Mom used to listen to the radio religiously anytime she was in the kitchen, so maybe it's the nostalgia of it that keeps me tuned to a few different stations I toggle between.

Paige found the old device at Upstairs Closet and was so proud when giving it to me, a treasure discovered among the rubble. Not like it's that hard to find a decrepit piece of technology in a thrift store, but that she knew how much this would mean to me.

She knows a lot of things like this.

And...there I go again.

Not obsessing over what could have been for the next few weeks is going to be hard. I'm realizing I have control over most things in my life except my feelings. They're unruly and want what they want. Paige is now fully hardwired into my brain, my cells, my fucking heart.

"I can do this," I breathe in. "Another day," I breathe out.

The shower is out to get me when I turn it on, and it gets too hot, only for me to overcorrect and make it way too cold. Lukewarm doesn't feel refreshing like it normally does after a hard workout, so I rinse off and quickly abandon the spray jets pelting my back. It's all wrong tonight. Maybe I should watch a show or take up knitting. God, who am I, my mother?

Toweled off and changed, I check my phone only to notice a missed call from Paige.

My stomach plummets to the floor below me. I saw her this morning before she left, but we haven't talked all day. Could something be wrong? Is she hurt?

Stop. It.

I'm overreacting. She's probably just fine and called to tell me not to forget to water the plants she doesn't have.

There's only one missed call instead of the fifty-eight she'd usually leave like she did when the reunion show of *Love is Blind* aired. I was on my way to her house and stopped at the grocery store to pick up the orange popsicles I know she likes, and even that was too long.

We ended up on FaceTime while I finished checking out before making my way to her house. She gave me a highly detailed account of everything everyone was saying, which was a lot. That's pretty much the whole point of that episode: blabbing. And I love every minute.

"She's probably just calling to check in," I tell myself as I click the missed call and try to reach her.

It rings for an ungodly amount of time, and I'm about to hang up when she finally answers, laughing. "Rhodes! Hi!"

Okay, not hurt.

"How are you? I must have missed your call while I was…at the gym."

I'll explain the pickleball thing later.

"I'm great," she says through another laugh.

What is so damn funny?

The edge I'm teetering on is only getting sharper and harder to balance.

"We're at a diner outside Spokane. There was a small, feathery issue, and Archie and Winnie stopped to help."

Who the fuck are Winnie and Archie?

Not even a minute into our conversation, and I already can't help feeling like I've missed out on too much these last couple of hours while I was getting demolished in pickleball. But I don't want to come across as overbearing or weird about her being with these strangers.

But I really don't like it.

"So, uh, Archie and Winnie? Those are some names," I say with a clipped laugh.

"They're the best," she touts. "We ordered pie for lunch, and I think they might be my new favorite people. They've been traveling in their RV full-time for *years*! Like, plural! Can you believe that?"

"I'm shocked," I say in the most monotone voice ever.

All I can think is Paige doing the same. Can Vincent VanGo even drive that far? I have my suspicions. Putting her on speaker, I pull up my local marketplace app with everything from used nail polish to used vehicles and run a quick search for other potential vans just in case Vincent dies a sudden and unexpected death. You can never be too prepared.

"I was, too," she says. "But they're retired, so there's that."

I clear my throat while scrolling. There's a sense of relief knowing they're at least older, but it still doesn't ease my mind that they could somehow be trying to take advantage of her. "Are you still planning to stop in Spokane tonight?"

"Yeah, I'm going to drive to my campground after this. Archie and Winnie said they'd follow me there since it isn't far from where they're staying in order to help me get things set up. Isn't that so nice of them?"

Absolutely not. Strangers bringing Paige to where she's staying—*alone*—so they can *help* her? What kind of help are they going to give?

"Are you sure that's a good idea?" I can't help myself. "You don't know these people very well, and they could be baiting you with their gray hairs."

"Of course it's a good idea. They want to help." Her normal sing-song voice lowers. "And I trust them."

I know she's trying to convince me of this, like I should trust them, too. I'm not sure if my tone or question clued her into the fact that I don't think she's being safe, but she picked up on it all the same.

"I'm a big girl, Rhodes."

Fuck. I'm screwing this up. But her safety is important to me. I love this woman and don't want anything to happen to her, including being lured in by the grandparent-type. My overprotective senses are on full alert when it comes to Paige. Everything inside my cells tells me to swoop in and save her. *Call the police!* my heart screams. But I'm still just the best friend. I need my heart and brain to work together to remember this.

"Tell them you have a sword in your van." *Okay.* I'm obviously not ready to think rationally. "You still have that knife Machete Lady gave you, right?"

"You mean the pocket knife?"

"Yes, that," I confirm with a snap of my fingers. "Tell them it's a sword though so they know you're armed."

"Rhodes, really?"

"Yes, really!" I yell louder than I intended. "You can't be too safe."

She huffs. "You know what? I have to go."

I know I'm fucking this up, and she's slipping away. But I just can't help it. Or at least explain to her that these feelings I've woken up inside me are strong and wild and so out of control, I don't know how to tame them. Maybe a whip or electric collar? Who the hell knows? Instead, I just resign myself to the fact I can't do anything. She isn't asking for my help.

I exhale and try again. "Tell them I say hi, and text me later when you're all settled if you want. No pressure. Or text Amber. Your Mom or Dad. Even Constance. Hell, add Machete Lady to the group text. Just someone."

"Okay, I will," she says, and it's like I can see her biting the inside of her cheek and twisting her lips.

I'm sure she thinks I'm being ridiculous.

I can't disagree.

She doesn't say goodbye, and if I didn't already know it was a Turner family habit, I would've felt worse about overstepping. Instead, I just feel mildly bad. I'll apologize the next time we talk or maybe grovel in a text if I can't sleep tonight.

I don't like this new dynamic. I'm more worried than usual, more overbearing. Unfortunately, I can't play pickleball. I just got back, and that might be overdoing it.

So, for now, in order to put a muzzle on my emotions, I grab my laptop from the coffee table and sit back on the couch. I should probably start editing my next video, but instead, I toggle to a new search bar and type in something I can control:

How to improve your pickleball game.

MY EYES ARE drooping closed, and my consciousness is between the worlds of awake and asleep.

My dad used to say he was *just resting his eyes*. That's me.

Until my phone buzzes.

I fling my eyes wide and pull my arms out of the burrito I created with my blanket in my bed to check my phone.

Paige:
> I'm alive.

I exhale deeply, relaxing back into my pillow. The racing thoughts keeping me from fully falling into a deep sleep ease up, and I sigh with relief.

Me:
> Would it be too much to ask for proof of life?

She sends a selfie of her feet outstretched in front of a roaring campfire. An elderly couple sits across from her in camp chairs that likely belong to them since Paige only brought one she found at Upstairs Closet. It's a fuzzy sphere-shaped bucket seat that could likely sit two. The thing took up too much space inside the van, so she strapped it to the back, refusing to leave it behind.

The thought makes me smile all over again as I study the brightness of the fire in her photo. An ache behind my ribs acts up again, which I don't think will entirely go away until she's back.

Paige:
> Now, where's your proof of life?

I smile to myself then hover the phone above me to snap a picture to send off to her. The flash turns on automatically, and I'm blinded by the intense light, squinting even more than I already was.

Paige:
> I can barely see you!

We can't have that.

I unravel myself even more and slip out of bed, like I wasn't just being lulled to dreamland, and flip on the light. I ruffle my hair, which might make it worse since some of it falls over my forehead, per usual, while the rest is sticking up at odd angles, but I take a picture anyway and send it. We never filter our selfies to each other, and I'm not starting now.

Paige:
> You were sleeping, weren't you?

Me:
> I was just resting my eyes.

Paige:
> Mhm.

Paige:
> I can always tell by your expression.

Me:
> And what does it tell you?

The three dots appear and disappear. I'm too wired to lay back down, so I prop myself in the corner of my small sectional Paige helped me pick out on Black Friday a couple of years ago. She only consented to purchasing a new one if it was on sale. Half off with free delivery was enough for her.

Paige:
> Your eyes are barely open, and you get this lazy grin. It's very you.

I'm smiling now, wondering if it's the kind she likes.

Me:
> I'm surprised you're not already in bed.

Paige:
> It's only 8.

Me:
> It's 9, and you've been driving all day.

Paige:
> I think the whole bird incident aged me by ten years minimum.

Me:
> Bird incident?

This must've been why she called earlier today.

Paige:
> I killed a bird today.

Paige:
> Don't worry, I'm fine. The bird is not.

She took the question right out of my fingers as I was typing it out.

Paige:

> I wrote about it in the journal you gave me while Winnie and Archie went to get pizza. You'll read about it when I get back.

Me:

> You're going to let me read your journal?

Paige:

> Maybe. I kind of just started writing like I was telling you the story. "Dear Rhodes" just felt right.

There isn't a chance in hell there's anything *lazy* about my grin now.

Me:

> I like that.

Paige:

> I wanted you to be a part of this trip as much as possible.

Of course, my time spent worrying about losing her to an elderly couple is obliterated by this comment. She sees me. Sees through all my worries that I'm being left behind, that we still have so much to talk about and process after our kiss, and understands my intense need to keep her safe.

But I'm starting to realize she can't figure out what she really wants while I keep her safe. There's a level of risk she's going to have to take.

Every great journey has some, including mine.

I'm starting to think mine is the risk of letting go. No one explained how I'd admit to having feelings for my best friend only to have to wave and smile as she left me. But maybe she hasn't left me completely like I thought.

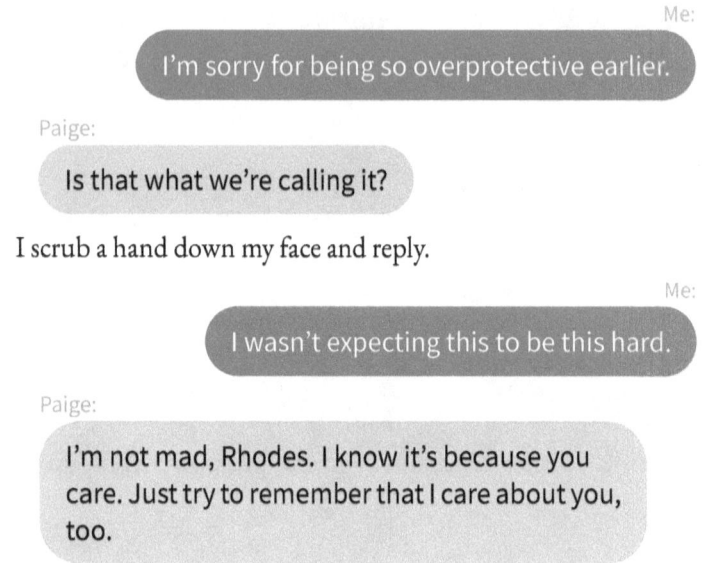

I scrub a hand down my face and reply.

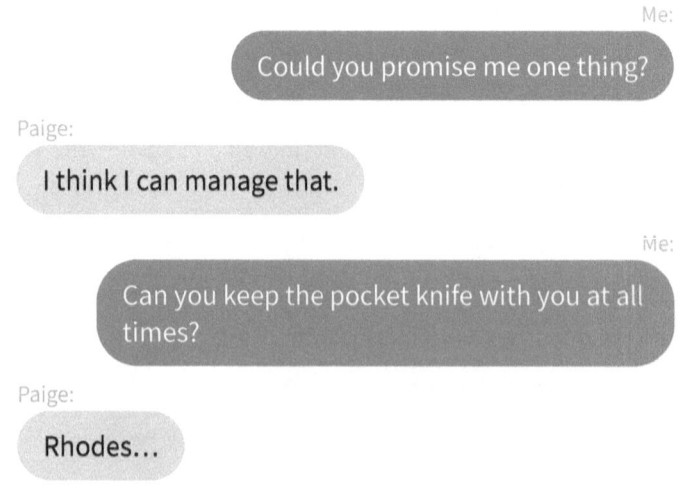

Her words aren't a promise or a confession of love, but they are what I needed to hear.

> **Me:** Okay, okay, sorry. Again.

> **Paige:** I promise.

My whole body relaxes.

> **Paige:** Now probably wouldn't be the right time to tell you that I don't actually know how to open it.

A smile tugs at my lips.

> **Me:** Call me tomorrow, and I'll show you.

Something tells me I'm going to have a lot of opportunities to get this right.

8

PAIGE

"I've tracked your GPS location," Mom says in a rush when she FaceTimes me.

I whisper an apology to Winnie and Archie. They nod, and I continue talking to Mom. "How do you even know how to do that?"

"The internet has a lot of tutorials," she responds, sounding slightly less flustered. "I can see you're at your campground now and not doing drugs."

I pause and tilt my head. "And how do you know that? Location tracking wouldn't show what I'm doing."

"Because I know you," she replies, a smile in her voice.

Winnie snickers behind a closed fist.

I huff a laugh. "So why'd you even ask—"

"Who was that?"

And, here we go again. Like it wasn't enough trying to convince Rhodes I'm fine with my new friends, now I have to convince Mom.

"Winnie and Archie are friends I met earlier. They're in their sixties, retired, have a Beagle, and enjoy traveling around the US in their fifth wheel. Would you also like their social security numbers?"

Mom's voice turns up. "No, but I'm not above a thumbprint."

"Mom," I say on a sigh. "I swear I'm okay."

She sighs, too. "I believe you. I'm just bummed I missed your call. And I miss you."

"I miss you, too."

We are barely through the first day, and this trip is completely open-ended, making it impossible to give any assurances. Maybe I want to spend more time in one spot or visit somewhere else. The timeline is vague. And I get it. We're a close-knit family and rarely spend long stretches away from each other. When Mom hugged me this morning as I left and handed me a stack of coupons along with dinner leftovers from the night before, I knew she'd be doing that sort of thing regardless of my age. They have always been there for me, maybe a little too much. I don't think they get that supporting me can also mean giving me *space*. It's a hard concept I've been trying to manage for years.

She smiles, but it's sad. "I picked up Carlos' pizza since I had to work later tonight—your favorite."

I press a hand to my heart. "I can smell the garlic crust from here."

"Swear you'll call if you need anything?"

"I swear."

She nods and then hangs up without another word.

"Sounds like you created quite a stir with the people you love?" Winnie phrases it as a question.

My mind skips over Mom and goes right to Rhodes. "I mean, yeah, I guess. When I called them earlier...after..."

She nods and waves her hand. "The dead bird. Got it."

"Yes. The bird," I confirm. "No one answered, which is weird and completely unlike my family. We're always calling or texting each other. Checking in and sending random tidbits of information that would mean nothing to anyone else but us...me, and I love it. I guess I just miss them. I'm sure that sounds pathetic coming from an almost thirty-year-old woman."

She chuckles. "Not at all. Family relationships are something special."

I tug the blanket I pulled from my bed higher on my lap. The fire flickers with orange and yellow lights, sometimes blue, while licking the air. It's peaceful out here, where nature is the loudest sound for miles.

Constance would likely shrivel up out here, seeing as she hates the cold almost as much as she hates when the yolk of her egg breaks. Mom and Dad would enjoy this, though. Looking up and seeing the host of stars flickering with light and existence, I know they'd have their necks craned back. Dad would likely have some joke about Orion's belt, and Mom would swat his shoulder while cackling.

It's times like this I remember how much I love having a close family. But it's also when I remember that it's okay to hoard a few of these life experiences for myself.

"They certainly are." I cross my ankles. "I haven't traveled out of the state a lot, either, so I guess I'm still figuring things out."

Winnie gasps. "You haven't?"

Archie appears halfway asleep with their Beagle, Dottie, stretched out across his feet. He doesn't even stir at her reaction.

I shake my head. "Never really had a reason to leave."

"So, why now, then? What changed?"

Me, I want to say. It's the truth, after all. But not all of it, and there's something about Winnie that makes me want to share everything with her. And possibly because I'm a chronic oversharer. "My friend Rhodes—the one I was talking to earlier—told me he had feelings for me."

Her mouth gapes, eyes widening. "You don't say."

I nod and purse my lips. "He told me a couple of weeks ago, and I think it just shook me up a bit. I wasn't expecting it, so I definitely didn't know what to do. We've always been friends, closer than I am with my own sister." I pause to think back to the parking lot moment when he kissed me like my lips were familiar and right and everything good. "I freaked out and decided I needed to get away." I wave a hand at Vincent VanGo behind me. "This was an impulse purchase."

Hearing myself tell the story out loud just confirms that maybe this wasn't the right decision. But at the time, it's what I had to work with. The Itch I'd been feeling for months leading up to this decision was enough to make me do *something*. I was either going to get a full-body tattoo, start another business, or take a trip.

At least it wasn't palm reading.

Winnie's brows relax. "How we start the journey is rarely how we end it, sugar."

My lips curl upward, and I sink further into my chair, watching the last sprigs of light fall behind the mountainscape as the sun says goodnight. "I hope not, since I started this journey by...you know." *Murder.* "I'm not sure I'm cut out for life on the road."

She glances at Archie whose head is tipped back, snoring lightly, then looks at me. "I didn't so much like the idea of living on the road, either, at first. But now I realize how much more it's given back to me. Time, adventure, awe," she says wistfully. "Those aren't things you can always pay for or even experience with a stagnant lifestyle."

I cross my legs and bounce my foot while I talk. "I want those experiences, too. It's why I didn't want to plan my stops ahead of time. I want to prove to myself that I can figure things out as I go and get to know who I am—what I really want—in the process."

"Those are big questions to answer," Winnie says. "Mostly because they change. Hell, I'm still trying to figure them out for myself."

"Yeah, I'm probably taking on too much, expecting more than is possible. I tend to do that. I just needed to do something, and feel some way. Anything different than repeating the same patterns."

She's quiet for a moment, letting a bit of my defeat take some of the space between our words.

"I'm ashamed to even admit this," I say in a hushed tone. "But I thought about driving home after the incident. I wasn't sure I even wanted to be by myself anymore. Not if it costs an animal its life. If you hadn't been there..." My thoughts trail off, then circle back to what's really plaguing my mind. Not the past or present, but the future. "Things could get worse."

She hums. "Isn't that the truth? Things could get worse. But they could also get better." She sits forward. "I'm going to tell you something I tell my own daughter."

I sit up a little but cross my arms to fend off the chill in the air.

"Whenever we reach for the good, there's bound to be some hard. They often go together. But that shouldn't stop us from going after the good, honey. You've got a lot ahead of you to look forward to, and I have no doubts you'll find what you're looking for." She swirls a finger in the air. "You're going to find it outside," she taps her chest, "and inside."

It's a wonder she can even hear me when I ask, "How can you be so sure?"

"Oh, I'm not. All I know is you've put yourself in the best position for it, and sometimes, that's all we can do. Open our palms and ask."

This time, when I smile, my face doesn't light up. It feels worn and soggy. But the resolve strengthening inside my chest is stronger somehow.

Maybe I can't do this, but I want to.

And I think that's a good enough start.

CURLING UP IN bed for the first night of sleep in Vincent isn't how I thought it would feel.

Not in terms of comfort. The bed is soft, and my comforter came directly from home, filled with down feathers and smelling like I expect it to. Cleo is already curled up on my pillow, tail falling across my shoulder.

Winnie and Archie left an hour ago after more rousing stories of roadkill, mechanical issues, and the weird campgrounds they've seen across America. I immediately came inside to eat dried mango and lock every door, feeling bone tired and ready to crawl into bed with my snack.

I decided to stay another day in Spokane and maybe check out the riverfront park I read so much about online, which means I have nothing else to think about. Nothing to worry over and nothing to distract me.

It's quiet, apart from the small fan I brought for white noise.

And I'm alone.

I don't have Taylor Swift's lyrics to keep me company while I drive or Winnie and Archie to assure me I'm just where I need to be.

It's just me again, staring at the ceiling that seems to be blinking back at me since the wallpaper with eyes continues from one end of the van to the other. I adjust under the blankets to try and relax since I'm lying like a Mummy in a coffin currently. The razor-sharp blades of hair on my legs scrape together while I flip onto my side and again when I flip to the opposite side.

That's it.

I'm never going to sleep.

Thoughts of Russel Crow aren't keeping me up. Winnie was right, and every time my mind drifts back to that moment, all I can think about is Cleo trying to dig him up again. It makes me smile, which is a level of dark humor I didn't think I was capable of.

Maybe I just can't sleep because Winnie's words still stand at attention in my mind as I rub my feet together, warming them from the chill of wearing flip-flops outside.

Whenever we reach for the good, there's bound to be some hard.

And hell, if she wasn't right. Today was mostly good with only a sprinkle of hard. I met new friends, reached the right campground, and laughed—a lot.

I can do this, but more importantly, I'm ready to.

So why do I feel scared? Like when you're expecting someone to jump out from around a corner and startle you into oblivion.

Reaching above my head, I carefully grab the notebook with my name etched into the front so I don't disturb Cleo. I pull off the pen I clipped to the front cover, ready to jot down important thoughts as I open to a blank page. Balancing the spine on my chest, I stare at the cream-lined pages, completely void and awaiting words I don't yet know.

It's a metaphor, I'm sure, and it makes me think of Winnie again—the wise older woman with things to say.

I don't know exactly what I want to write or how I want to share the thoughts and feelings swirling inside, but I know how I want to start this one.

I touch the ballpoint to the page and write:

Dear Rhodes.

9

Paige

Dear Rhodes,

I almost drove home today.

I didn't tell you this on the phone earlier, but I wanted to turn right around after killing a bird with my front bumper. There were still feathers stuck in the grill when I got to my campsite (cue whole body shudder). I'll spare you the rest of the morbid details, but I can officially say I've attended a funeral for roadkill.

Please stop laughing.

I'm serious!

I know what you're thinking, but you have to know this was terrifying. I've never killed anything. You know, I'd rather safely capture a spider I find inside to release it back into the wild than take a shoe to it. It was scarring in a way that first-time experiences can be, and I guess that's why it feels big: because I'm still here.

I'm still reaching for good, even when it's hard.

I still want whatever this adventure brings.

I'm open to it changing my mind.

And I really hope it does.

Yours,

Paige

10

PAIGE

I was hit by a truck.

Or so it feels like waking up this morning. My arm is propped at an odd angle above my head, and all of the blood has rushed out of it, leaving me with nothing more than a pool noodle to hit snooze. That might be why I knocked the small cloud-shaped alarm to the floor.

And my foot is in my sink.

Wait...what?

I lift my head just enough to see my foot in the small stainless sink built into the cabinetry beside the end of my bed. Just lovely.

My arm tingles while I hang it off the side of the bed, so the blood rushes back. I groan loudly, still listening to the upbeat electronica music I chose to get me pumped to wake up in the morning.

Consider me enthusiastic.

Not.

"Cleo, turn it off."

She stretches her paws out across my stomach, saying nothing.

I still reply like she did. "I know you don't know how, but please?"

I'm talking to my cat, which would be weird for anyone who isn't an animal lover, but to me, it's completely normal. I have conversations with her every day. I imagine how she'd respond, and I think this fits because there is no way she'd ever get out of bed before me.

She sprawls across my stomach like she's getting comfy again. Not helping.

The pinpricks in my arm have lessened, and my foot is starting to get cold from resting it in the sink.

I peel the covers off me, and Cleo quickly scurries off to find another resting place at the end of the bed. Pulling my legs in, I use whatever's left of my weak abs to sit up. I'm like a corpse rising from the dead. I feel like I've slept like the dead, too, in the strain of my neck and tightness in my shoulders. I suppose falling asleep upright for the first half of the night while journaling will do that.

I slide off the edge and pick up my alarm clock, finally getting some relief, and turn it off. *Silence.* My ears are still ringing slightly, but my body comes back online, as I stretch every limb out or up.

My hand flops around on the shelf above my pillow without the help of my eyes to look for my glasses. When I find them, I shove them on my face and wince when I slam my palm into my nose. I yelp and curse myself for doing this too often as someone who has worn glasses her whole life.

There's a humming sound coming from outside that steals the quiet once again, except this time, I'm instantly curious since it's right outside my van. When I arrived last night, there weren't any other campers, and I wondered why I was the only one. But peeling back the blue corduroy curtains, matching the rest of the blue in this vehicle, I spy a few other campers and a much nicer van next to me.

This one is white and sleek, with a top rack and a bike hanging off the back. The woman who must have been humming comes around to the driver's side door of her vehicle to put something away, and I'm met with a wave of nostalgia.

Her bright red highlights remind me of Delia, my ex-coworker from Upstairs Closet Thrift. She's the one who recommended I do the blind dating experiment, leaving me with a best friend who admitted his feelings for me. But seeing this person with dyed red hair gives me a rush of homesickness.

What a way to wake up.

I shake my head and brush off the memories.

For now, I need to figure out how to make coffee in a van.

I let the curtain fall closed and squat low to open the cabinet under the sink to assess the water situation. I wish I knew the specifics of how the tank worked, but I wasn't really listening when Dad was explaining it. I see the water, but how do I get it out? There are no valves, hoses, or spigots that I can see, and I start to worry.

I could call Dad and ask, but giving in to this urge feels like I'd somehow be failing.

"Cleo, did you hear what he said?" I flip the handle on the sink. No water. I sigh. "Maybe it's outside."

I grab a thick sweater with small bows stitched into it and slip on a pair of Birks I scored at Upstairs Closet before heading outside in my flannel pajamas. I'm just hoping the people at this campground have seen worse. I note the woman is no longer near her driver's side door, so I slip around the other side of my van to start looking for a valve.

There's a screw top cap that's in the same area as the water tank under my sink just outside, but upon opening it, I'm positive this is only for filling it. At least I'll know that for later.

The woman is humming again, so I peep around the back of my van to see what she's up to now. There's a small fire in the pit with a hanging kettle over it and a grill of some sort stretched from one side to the other with a cast iron pan on top.

Bacon.

The familiar sizzle and crackle are making my stomach knot with hunger pains. My mouth waters as she starts flipping them over. It doesn't appear like there's anyone else with her. She's alone, like me, but wholly more prepared for camping with an outdoor trash bin, a pop-up wash station complete with a drying rack on the picnic table, and a folding table to rest utensils on. The one chair she has looks like it's from the future with two legs she has to balance on, planting her feet into the ground as the other chair legs.

Her gaze drifts toward my van, doing a double take when she sees me peeking. I yank my head back, but I guarantee it wasn't fast enough. She saw me.

"Care for some bacon?" she calls out.

I inwardly and outwardly cringe, knowing she saw me watching her. But what am I supposed to do now? I can't just deny her offer. It looked like a lot of bacon, and she probably couldn't eat it all on her own.

I poke my head back out, and the rest of my body follows. "Good morning."

She tips her chin, a knowing glint in her eye. "Morning."

I can already tell she's far cooler than I am with her red hair, water-resistant pants that zipper at the knees, and hiking boots with legit tread. But I still walk tentatively toward her five-star camping resort, hooking a thumb over my shoulder. "I wasn't spying. I was just trying to figure out my water and smelled bacon. No one was in this spot when I got here last night."

"I'm Penny." She quickly scans my flannel pants and mismatched sweater, then gestures toward another space chair I hadn't noticed. "Got in late last night. Drove up from Oregon."

"Paige." I give a small wave and then lift the chair, assessing how I'm supposed to sit. "Is that where you're from?"

"No," she states then uses a pair of tongs to move the bacon around. "I'm from Maine."

I squat down like I'm doing wall sits, my legs quivering while I hold the back of the chair in one of my hands, hoping it will catch me in this trust fall. "Did you drive all that way?" I ask, looking far less graceful than her as I try to sit, then bail at the last second.

She smiles, then stands to walk over and hold the back of the chair for me. "That's it. Just sink right down and keep your feet grounded in order to stay balanced."

I'm falling back, holding my legs at a perfect ninety-degree angle and trusting her and this futuristic chair despite them being strangers.

When she realizes I won't fall backward, she returns to sit with ease. "I've been on the road for a year, going slowly from place to place and stopping wherever I feel like it. I'm planning to winter somewhere in the south and figure this was a good time to visit the north before the snow hits."

"A year?" I don't mean to sound aghast, but I'm just over twenty-four hours into this thing and just now starting to believe in people like her, Winnie, and Archie, living life on the road. it's not like I'm seeing Bigfoot for the first time.

She laughs and plucks the bacon from the pan, depositing it on a plate. "It doesn't feel like it's been that long at all. Life on the road is slower, but time still ticks."

I nod like I understand this completely.

"How long have you been traveling?" she asks, offering me the plate.

I carefully take a slice of bacon and then decide two is always better, but I have to bounce it around in my hands since it's still so hot. "Since yesterday. It's why I was trying to figure out my water."

"You have a tank?"

I bite into the bacon and swear it's the best I've ever eaten, perfectly crispy. "Yeah, I can see the tank under the sink, but I don't know how to get the water out. I'm sure that probably sounds ridiculous. Maybe you're thinking: *Why would you drive across multiple states when you don't know how to get water?*" I mime this with wild hand motions, looking more like I'm doing the robot than anything.

She takes a bite, chewing as she says, "You'd be surprised what you can learn just by doing something. You're forced to figure it out."

"I guess you're right since I'd probably be willing to offer my left arm just to make a cup of coffee."

She laughs. "I can help."

Hope swells in my chest. "Really?"

Her brows lower. "Of course. That's what neighbors do."

She stands swiftly, walking toward my van before I've even stood. Let's be real...rolling out would have been a generous description.

PENNY FIGURED OUT the issue in less than a minute.

I only had time to look down at my phone and back up before the problem was fixed, and my sink was spitting out a decent stream of liquid.

She pushes from her knees to a squat, pointing at the turn dial I must have missed in my haste to figure it out. "It's just a valve you need to turn whenever you want to use it, and your vehicle is parked. Don't forget that part; you could spring a leak and have a bigger problem to handle." Cleo bumps up against her leg, and she pets my friendly feline before standing.

"Did you build out the interior?" I'm still a little bit in shock when she waves a finger around the cramped space.

I snicker while grabbing a mug from my upper cabinet. "No, definitely not. I bought it like this and added a few design touches."

"It looks great for the age of the vehicle."

"Thanks." Pride bubbles up in my chest at hearing this. Maybe I didn't pick a total loser to travel part of the country with. It's validating.

"Do you know how to flush your waste system?"

I stare at Penny blankly, then realize what she's referring to. "Oh! No. I don't have a bathroom in here."

"What about your gray water?"

I shake my head since I had no idea water came in colors.

She laughs and packs up the small toolkit she brought over. "The water that you use in your sink. Sometimes food gets in there and turns the water—"

"Gray!" I say with a snap of my fingers.

"Yeah," she confirms. "There's usually a tank that holds this water, and you want to make sure to flush it regularly."

That makes a lot of sense and would probably be good information to know.

Seeing the panic rising on my face, she adds, "I could show you how to do it if you want. Maybe a few other things that might be helpful to know, too?"

I practically jump on her when I circle her in a surprise hug. "Yes! Thank you! I will pay you, if you want, or name my firstborn child after you. I love the name Penny—"

"No need," she says with a friendly pat on the back. "This is exactly how I learned—asking people at every stop and gaining a little more with every conversation. Oh, and the internet. But you could help me hem a couple of curtains."

I pull away, and she tips her head to my sewing machine sitting behind the passenger seat I snuck in when Amber and Rhodes weren't looking. As a seamstress, curtains are the number one thing I've been asked to sew over the years. I could stitch them together with my eyes closed, which I probably shouldn't do.

It's an easy answer that makes me feel like a bartering goddess. "Done."

11

RHODES

"Why are you so good at this?" Amber asks through strained breaths.

I stare at her across the net, breathing hard while my paddle hangs at my side. Did I just black out while playing?

"I-I don't know." Except, I do know.

I've been spending most of my free time these past two days watching videos to avoid spending most of that time thinking about Paige. It's working. But that also means I've watched a lot of matches and learned tips and tricks to improve my game and form.

"I've been studying." I shrug.

Her mouth gapes. "No. You're obsessed."

There's probably a little bit of obsession sprinkled in there, too. "I like pickleball."

"It's terrible."

"Because you haven't hit your stride yet."

She glares at me. "No, it's because you've become a professional overnight. You're athletically built, and I enjoy eating muffins. How are we supposed to face Jim and Agnes now?"

I shrug again and adjust the sweatbands on my wrists I found for a great deal at the sporting goods store yesterday. "We play. We win."

She crosses her arms and nods. "You've been converted to the dark side."

"To what?"

"To a highly obsessed sports person!" she yells, throwing her hands in the air. "Your brain has been hijacked by team spirit and endorphin rushes that only last as long as a game. You're probably going to start hosting watch parties at your house every week. Well, I'm only going to come if there are snacks. *Good* snacks. Not beetroot salad or something."

I shift on my feet, examining the feel of the rackett in my hand. "Beetroot salad is delicious, by the way. Something you'd know if you actually tried it. And you make it sound like being a sports person is the worst thing that could happen."

"It basically is."

"I haven't thought about Paige all morning."

She squints. "You texted her before we started playing."

"How'd you know that?"

She sighs, pinching the bridge of her nose. "Because you get this specific look on your face anytime you think or even mention her. It's curious and attentive, with your raised brows and sly smile. A little desperate if you ask me."

I throw my hands wide. "I *am* desperate, Amber. That's why I started playing this in the first place."

It's not like I wanted a new hobby, but it's basically programmed into me. When Dad had his stroke, I started dabbling in videography more seriously to have something that wasn't tainted by talks of his progress or the lack of it.

Now, it's my career.

She stalks closer to the net separating us. "Thinking about her isn't the problem here."

This is news to me. "I thought that was the exact problem."

She shakes her head. "You need to do what Paige is doing and go on a self-discovery journey inside your heart and mind. Why didn't you tell her how you felt for years? Why'd you lie to her? What is it about Paige you love so much?"

Her finger is pointed at my chest by the end of her rant, crossing the line of the net and stabbing through to my core. She's right, of course. Amber is usually the friend in our trio who is the most observant. It's why she is so much better at search-and-find puzzles than we are.

Rounding the net and stalking toward the bench, she sets her racket down and sits with a thud. "And while you're at it, ask yourself, *why pickleball?*"

It doesn't feel like the right moment to mention that she suggested it.

I don't walk as fast to meet her on the bench, but when I make it there, I sit beside her and grab my water bottle. I've been avoiding thoughts of Paige for the last couple of days because thinking about her means considering all the ways I've messed up. The reality of my crush is that it actually ended up hurting her *and* me. That isn't what I intended, but it was the impact I had.

"How do I fix this?" I ask in a small voice.

She blows out a breath. "You start being honest with yourself. With Paige. With me."

My brows quirk together. "Not that I don't disagree on the whole, but what do I need to be honest with you about?"

She swivels her head to the side and glares at me through a squint. "Do you really like pickleball?"

A small smile pulls at my lips. "I do."

She groans. "Dammit."

"It's okay if you don't, Amber."

She leans against the glass wall at our backs. "I won't let you compete against Jim and Agnes by yourself. I'll be there on Saturday. And every other day you want to practice. But you have to promise me something."

I stare at my hands. "What?"

"Ask yourself the hard questions, Rhodes, and be the man Paige needs."

There isn't a script for this sort of thing. I'm not even sure where to start other than being honest with myself first. I want something real with Paige. I want her to know I'm not going to lie about my feelings or what I'm thinking about—which mostly includes her. I want her to be able to rely on me like she's never been able to with all of the other *boys* she's dated.

I want all of that and so much more.

When I bought Paige her journal, I got a second one for myself to use for work. The leather was nice, and the pages were simply lined, making it an easy yes. Instead of using it for work, though, maybe I should do the same thing Paige is doing and write my thoughts down on paper—be honest in a way that gives me space to think.

Yeah, I think I'll do that.

"Thanks, Amber," I say. "I needed that."

"I know."

I rest my elbows on my knees and peer at her.

There's a smirk on her face. "Now," she starts, looking at her watch, "we have fifteen more minutes to play before my chiropractic appointment."

I push to stand and offer her a hand. "You're really taking full advantage of this guest pass, aren't you?"

She strides to the court. "I'm thinking about joining."

"No, you're not."

She whips around and crouches in position, ready to receive the ball. "You're right, I'm not. But I'm going to enjoy using your gym for as long as possible."

I shake my head and step inside the square box, positioning the ball to serve to her. "Loser buys ice cream?"

It looks as though she won't agree, knowing she'll likely lose, but a new wave of confidence lights up her face. "You're on."

AFTER AMBER LOST horribly, I told her I'd cash in on the ice cream another day. I was eager to sit in the sauna and stretch my muscles, followed by some collaboration emails I had to respond to. It was exactly what I needed.

Grabbing my soap, I nimbly walk toward the showers since I forgot my sandals, then test the water for the perfect post-sweat temperature—lukewarm—and hang my towel. The stream of water hits my loosened shoulders, rushing down the planes of my body. I shiver at how refreshing it feels to sweat from exertion and the sauna before washing it all down the drain.

Amber's words come back to me with the force of the water pressure. *Be honest with Paige. Be honest with yourself.*

Two weeks ago, I was finally honest with Paige about how I felt, and those feelings haven't changed. I still want to be with her. To continue sharing all of the small things like watching our favorite shows, bringing her food, and hunting for treasures at the thrift store.

But if I'm being honest with myself, I also want the kind of vulnerability that comes from being in a committed relationship. I want this to be my last relationship, and I'm sure I could spend multiple journal pages just telling her why. I just don't know if she's there, too.

My parents are the epitome of their marriage vows, loving one another in sickness and health. In the moments where they aren't at their best. I want this.

I want this with Paige, and I know she's said she wants this, too. I felt it in the way she kissed me.

Maybe that's why I told her I loved her the day before she left. It's in me, welling up like the romantic I want to be. So if we have forever, isn't this time apart just a short moment in our story?

Tipping my head back into the water, it hits my hairline and the overspray showers my face.

She pulled back when I tried opening up and telling her how I felt. And it's likely because I've had years to think and feel this way. These feelings might be new to her. The ones I've only heard in the way she kissed me. She hasn't exactly said she likes me. I shove this thought aside. Curling back in on myself and acting as though I don't care as much as I do won't help even if I'm tempted.

There was a time in my life when nothing else mattered except Dad getting better. My feelings, wants, needs, were all put aside to focus on what he needed. For good reason, but I can't revert back to this mindset. My feelings matter. But what am I supposed to do with them while Paige is figuring hers out?

It's not like I can tell them to sit on the couch, and I'll be back to fetch them when it's time. Instead, they're just bouncing around in there without a soft place to land.

No wonder I feel restless.

I need to do something with all of this pent-up emotion, this desire anytime I think about her lips on mine. I know she felt something. The way her body pressed flush to mine, how her hands gripped my face, and her mouth opened, inviting me in to stay awhile. Those were *all* real despite the time and distance fooling me otherwise.

I rake rough fingers through my hair as my mind wanders to what Paige is doing right now. Up until an hour ago, I would have forced myself to think of something else, but instead, I linger here.

Maybe she's walking around downtown, stopping for a late lunch since it's almost after two. Or she forgot to eat, which is more likely, and she is walking along the river. Could she be packing up her campsite for her next stop in Idaho? Knowing Paige, she might have even taken a nap. When she texted this morning saying she felt sleep-drunk, I figured she'd be in bed early tonight. She always is when she gets *too* much sleep, something I haven't quite worked out yet.

The water pelts my chest as I turn to face it. Maybe she's doing other things. I didn't mean to, but I carried a bin of miscellaneous items outside when we were packing up the van. It included things like chapstick, hand lotion, pens, and a toy—the kind that vibrates.

Has she used it yet?

Probably not.

But the thought alone has me growing harder.

I'm glad my gym has private showers, and at this hour, I'm the only one in the locker room, tucked away behind a curtain and thinking about the woman I love using her vibrator. Maybe this is how I get rid of some of these feelings.

My hand trails between my thighs of its own volition, wrapping around my shaft like I've done many times before. But this time, I think of the vibrator. I think of Paige. I think of her using it, me using it with her, and I can't stop the train of my thoughts, chugging along like a steam engine that takes miles to slow down.

I tug on my erection, using my thumb to trail over the tip. It forces a hard breath out of me, and I have to prop my hand on the tiled wall, the water pelting my back. There's something about the dim lights, solace, and thoughts of Paige that push me to keep going. I grope from base nearly to the tip and back again.

Paige's lips on mine invade my thoughts, and I shudder. The way her body felt pressed against mine, and I imagine what it would be like if we didn't stop at one kiss. If we'd kept going, kept kissing and touching, groping and fondling one another. I imagine what her perfect breasts would feel like in my hands, and my cock surges, building to a length I know I won't last with.

Hand still pressed to the tile, my body pitches forward as I pump my hand faster, and I think about Paige's body under mine. As if my hand is really just the tight walls of her body circling me with a grip that tells me to stay and never leave.

My breathing quickens as I think of her legs wrapped around my waist, ankles hooked at my lower back as I push into her one thrust at a time. The surge in my body reaches its peak, and with sloppy motions, my orgasm rips through me as Paige's lips part, her head tips back, and she falls apart with me.

In my thoughts, at least.

I drop my hand from the shower wall, letting the last of my orgasm rush down the drain and already missing the feel of something I've never had. I open my eyes, realizing I shut them at some point, and Paige is gone. She isn't beneath me, beside me, or anywhere close to me.

And while thoughts of her are nowhere near the real thing, it's all I've got.

But the intensity burning a hole through my heart is still there.

Maybe even stronger now.

12

PAIGE

I knew something was wrong the moment my feet touched the paved ground at my new camping spot.

It's a state campground with spaces for small RVs and vans—like mine—and plenty of open grassy areas for the tent enthusiasts. I dropped my payment in a wooden box on the bulletin board as I drove in and chose a spot that I *thought* would be the best. But really, I don't think *best* exists here.

I only had to drive about forty minutes, but I'm already exhausted. Likely because I'm waving my hand around in the air above my head, swatting at bees that think I'm made of honey.

I'm not.

It's probably closer to Sriracha.

I nearly trip over the leg of a picnic table as I twirl around in circles, clutching Cleo to my chest while I try to decipher where I parked. Since I don't have a reliable bathroom in the van—the trash bag toilet is only for emergencies—I had to brave the great unknown of bee country just to make it to the vault toilet on the other side of the campground. The path was anything but straight, even with my eyes open. There was a bridge, potholes, and gravel with large rocks ripe for tripping,

And the website did *not* mention anything about bees.

They only showed scenic photos with the Coeur d'Alene Lake in the background, mountains, and colors so vibrant they span most of the color wheel. The babbling brook running somewhere behind my camp spot that feeds the lake appeared refreshing, as exhibited in the JPEG photos, but is nothing more than a cesspool for these pesky, flying creatures.

"Hold on, Cleo!" I swat around us, feeling bees hit my palms with every swipe as though I'm swimming in a pool of them. "We're almost there!"

Except now they're multiplying as we pass the trash can with a special lid I couldn't quite figure out because it's meant to keep bears out, and apparently me, too.

I think one of them touched my lip when I opened my mouth to scream.

It only makes me run faster, but they can fly, those sly little bastards!

And there are *so many* of them. Are they hatching—or whatever bees do—and multiplying in the air?

Did they call all of their bee friends to pester me?

The van is in sight, so I run.

I run like I'm being chased by a bear.

I run like there's an entire colony chasing me.

I run like I want to live to see another day.

Flinging the door open, I toss Cleo in first, knowing she'll land on her feet, and hop inside after her. I almost slam the door on my foot in order to avoid letting any bees inside with me, but it looks like we managed to escape them. The buzzing has quieted, but my ears are still ringing.

"We survived." I swing my gaze to Cleo as she licks her lips with a slow blink.

Unfortunately, she didn't go to the bathroom. She got her harness and leash on without even getting a chance to climb one of the many trees taunting us from the windows of the van, either.

I undo her harness. "Sorry, girl. We'll wait until the sun goes down. Maybe the bees are just really bad at this time of day."

It's only three o'clock.

I can tell this is going to be a one-night stop. Tomorrow, I'll move on from here the second the sun is up. But it still bums me out. Did I mention the views I was supposed to be enjoying? The mountains look different through a van window than being outside and staring up at them.

I'm probably just hangry. I haven't had lunch yet, but the adult macaroni and cheese—which isn't *really* a thing; it's all the same—I brought is going to have to wait since I still need to hook up the van to power. And that is outside, with the bees. I'll have to wrap a scarf around my face and put my sunglasses on just to brave it.

Nope.

Not a chance.

"Tuck in, Cleo, I don't think we're going to be getting out anytime soon." Maybe I should quickly search for another campsite instead of waiting until tomorrow. Practical me does not like this idea since I've already put cash into the small drop box at the entrance. I'd be losing money, and that just isn't an option. "We're going to have to suffer through the night."

I say that while I can quite literally hear the bees buzzing through the walls.

Grabbing a granola bar and a beef stick, I hop onto my bed, pushing aside the sky-blue window coverings I didn't have a chance to replace before embarking. Maybe I could stop at a thrift store and find some spare fabric to make my own. Penny's ended up looking perfect. The ones she bought were too long, so we took them up a little, and she couldn't have been happier. Meanwhile, she mapped out my entire electrical system on a piece of paper that I now have hanging on the wall like a piece of art.

She also provided me with her number in case I ran into something and needed help.

I don't think that included fumigation.

Bees hit the window from outside, searching for food like the little savages they are. "I have nothing!" I holler at them, though the jerky stick in my left hand would say otherwise.

I sigh and grab my phone while Cleo decides to eat the rest of her dry food and curl up in the driver's seat. My bed welcomes me as I lay back.

I haven't heard from Rhodes all day. Or Amber, for that matter, except for the GIF she sent with a dancing pickle holding some sort of paddle. I didn't get it, and I've spent an exceptional amount of minutes thinking about it today.

My parents have been good about calling each night to confirm I'm alive while Constance lurks in the background of the video call like she's the girl from *The Ring*, trying to freak me out.

She does.

But it's still hours from when I typically hear from anyone because they have *jobs*. That thing that keeps them occupied for most daytime hours. It's been precisely twenty-two days since I had one of those, and I'm all too aware of this. I'm no closer to knowing what I want to do for the rest of my life. All I can think about is some kind of office job behind a desk that comes with a device to suck the life out of you a little bit more every day.

But maybe I need to get a grown-up job like this for once. Everything else I've done has ended in disaster.

I can feel Cleo judging me. I'm positive she can read my mind even from across the van. "Don't look at me like that. I'll eventually figure it out. Taking a month off work isn't going to kill me."

Her direct stare would say otherwise.

I scroll through my phone for a while, avoiding the inevitable when I finally open the text string with Rhodes. It feels like I just talked to him this morning when I wrote in my journal, but it lacked one key element of a conversation: a response.

Me:
> Turns out you can die from too many bee stings.

Expecting him to respond right away probably isn't healthy. It's just that he usually does. So when I have to wait fifteen minutes, I swear I'm one hundred years old. I've also gone on a deep dive through the dark web of mutant bees who will probably live through the apocalypse.

Rhodes:
> Is this another random thing you learned from the internet? Or are you stating this from experience?

Me:
> If it was from experience, I'd be texting you from beyond the grave.

Rhodes:
> Not impossible.

God, I miss him. The way my mind and body remember the comfort he brings to my life is instant. The way he already knows my muchness without me needing to explain it away.

> **Me:** My ghost is here to warn you.
>
> **Rhodes:** Consider me warned.
>
> **Me:** The internet had a lot to say on the matter, but also this campground I booked is infested with bees. Cleo and I are going to be stuck in the van all night.
>
> **Rhodes:** I'm glad I packed you that deck of cards then.
>
> **Me:** What???? Where?
>
> **Rhodes:** Check the cabinet above the sink.

I push up to my knees and crawl to the end of my bed, lifting the small cabinet door up and shuffling through the random items I shoved up here. Lighters, paracord, a small tin of sewing supplies, and…a deck of cards with cats playing poker on the back of them.

> **Me:** You just saved me.
>
> **Rhodes:** You're welcome.
>
> **Me:** What are you up to?

I drop back to sitting and open up the cards, fanning them while I inhale. It isn't a pleasant smell, but it's familiar. I love playing cards, and Rhodes knows this since I often force him and Amber to play with me. It's the best when you're bored: fun, mentally stimulating, and can be played solo or with others. There are so many variations like King's Corners, Go Fish, Rage, and Poker...the list quite literally *never* ends.

Rhodes:

> I was just finishing up some edits on my latest video. The Legos are going camping.

Me:

> Timely.

Rhodes:

> That's what I thought.

Rhodes:

> I might need to hear about these bees for inspiration. FaceTime?

I can't explain why my stomach swoops like I'm freefalling on a rollercoaster, but it does. And I don't want it to stop.

This is *new* and also kind of great.

I tap his contact and start the video call, propping my phone on the stray accent pillow shaped like lips.

He answers before the phone even rings. "Your face isn't swollen, and you don't have small bandaids all over your body. That's a good sign."

I smile at the teasing lilt of his voice, coupled with the way he's trying to tame the hair falling over his forehead. "That's because I've been stung in places I can't show on camera."

"Who says?"

We really just dove right in, huh? "Because Cleo would never forgive me."

Thankfully, he changes the topic. "And how is Miss Cleocatra?"

"She's ignoring me," I say, leaning back against my propped pillow, giving her side-eye. "I told her we were going hunting, and then...bees. She's full of judgment and despair."

"I'm sure she'll forgive you if you give her a few of the treats I stashed in the glove compartment," he says as if this is nothing.

But it's *something*.

My mouth falls open with a gasp. "You didn't!"

"I did."

I sit up and slide off the bed, taking only a few steps before I'm seated in the passenger seat and holding up a bag of treats in front of the camera. Cleo is clamoring into my lap to try and get at them before I've opened the bag.

"You might just be her new favorite person now," he says with a wide smile.

I feign shock with another gasp. "Are you saying I wasn't already?"

"These are my secret weapon. She loves them, so I always keep a stash with me."

Hearing this makes my entire body light up, especially the organ in my chest, and I'm ready to promise Rhodes just about anything. Except I probably shouldn't. I'm a professional at offering all of myself up front. But I want to learn to keep things chill with Rhodes, grow our relationship at a natural pace like normal humans do.

I clear my throat and sit back in the passenger seat after offering Cleo her prized treats. All is forgiven. "What have you been up to lately?"

He leans back against his couch, his preferred office. "A lot of pickleball."

"Pickleball?" *Ah*. This explains Amber's GIF. "Like tennis?"

"It's different," he says, being evasive.

I prop the phone in one of the cupholders. "Come on. I want to hear all about it. Like I didn't even leave."

He pauses for a minute, studying me through the phone while I dart back to the bed for my cards, shuffling them and waiting for him to continue. I know what he's thinking: *but you did leave*. Fair. I did, but is it so wrong to still want to go on a self-guided discovery journey while knowing every little thing happening in his life?

Okay, I see the point.

He rests his forearm on top of his head. "It's just something I started in order to keep my mind off the fact you're gone." A pause that could fill a swimming pool follows. "And I miss your couch."

"My couch?"

He exhales. "Watching shows with extra legroom on mine is weird."

"Are you saying my couch is small?" I prod.

"I definitely am."

"It's not that small."

"Maybe not for someone of average height." He sucks in a breath, his chest rising. "The pickleball is working, though. Except for the part I can't play all day and night."

"That's...revealing." So is the fact I want to curl myself against his chest right now, tucking my head in the curve between his neck and shoulder. "Is there anything else you miss?"

I know I'm asking for trouble, but my heart doesn't heed the warning. It wants the torture of knowing he misses me, not just my perfectly sized couch.

He shakes his head. "I mean, sitting on your couch without you there wouldn't be as fun. You're my favorite person to watch trashy TV with."

I know for a fact I'm also the *only* one he watches trashy TV with. Amber is strictly a documentary person, especially those of the nature variety. But it feels like there is more he wants to say, and I wish he would just tell me the *more*, which is that he clearly misses me. I know I was the one who put physical distance between us, maybe a dash of the emotional kind, too, but I don't like it.

It's a new feeling coating the inside of my gut that makes me want a deeper connection. I'm desperate in a way I haven't been when it comes to him. The kiss we shared unlocked so much in so little time that I don't know how to categorize all these desires inside me. They are new but also like a favorite shirt you center your laundry schedule around, so you can wear it again as soon as possible. The one that fits like it was made for you and highlights all of your good features with its color and shape.

This is how Rhodes makes me feel.

My mouth is already opening and saying words I can't take back, but I don't think I want to. "I miss you, Rhodes."

His expression softens, lips curling into my favorite lazy smile. "I miss you, too."

It's like my heart takes a full breath, and I smile back. "I don't know what this is supposed to be like," I admit to him. "You and me."

"I don't either. I'm out of my depth here."

I blow out a sigh. "This is all so new. How you feel, how I feel. But, if I'm honest with myself and you...I like you, Rhodes. I don't want us to hide how we feel. Maybe we can just tell each other what we're thinking and try this thing out together."

"And this thing is..."

I clear my throat. "Dating. Long distance, of course. But we can try it out and see how it feels, you know?"

What just came out of my mouth?

Am I really suggesting this right now? I can't help but nervously pick at my fingers, feeling all sorts of exposed by my own suggestion. Where did that come from? I went from *I miss you* to *let's date*.

He nods slowly, chewing the inside of his cheek. "As the one who spent years hiding my true feelings from you, I get this. There really is nothing I want more than to tell you exactly how I feel. But right now is your time, Paige—your moment—and I don't want to get in the middle. We have time for dating."

Time is annoying.

You did this, a condemning voice says in my mind.

"What if I don't want to wait?" With the words out of my mouth, I wish I could reel them back and pretend they didn't happen because I sound so impatient and whiny.

"I'm sorry," I say quietly, without giving him a chance to respond.

I'm doing what I've always done with guys: rush. But this is Rhodes. I put space between us for a reason, and it's because, deep inside, I know I want to do it the right way. I want to stretch out in the truth that he loves me and let my feelings catch up.

"Why are you sorry?" he asks, sympathy lacing his question.

"I'm doing it again. Rushing into a relationship." The confession feels weird to say out loud. I've never called attention to my serial dating.

"No, you're not."

I meet his eyes through the screen, close but still hundreds of miles away. "Rhodes, I'm ready to ask you to be my boyfriend after telling you I wasn't ready and fleeing the state."

He groans. "Don't remind me, or I'm going to throw away my resolve and make you mine. I'm more helpless when it comes to you than I think you know."

He is?

It's so new hearing him say these kinds of things unguarded. A thrill runs through me at just how good it feels and how eager I am for him to keep going. But he's right; I'm on this journey to find the me I want to become, and it's probably normal to want to revert back. But not this time. Not with Rhodes.

"I won't let you," he says with a sureness I don't have. "Not until you feel ready."

I lean against the seat and pull my knee up to rest my chin. "And how do I know when I'm ready? What if this trip doesn't fix me? What if I'm not *ready* for years?"

He pushes up and leans forward over his knees. "I'm not going anywhere."

"You say that now."

"I've liked you for years. Trust me when I say that won't change today, tomorrow, or years down the road. If that's what it takes, what you need, I'll be here."

Tears push at the backs of my eyes, and I know deep inside the code of my DNA that this man, my Rhodes, is everything he says. He is true and loyal, open and patient.

He's my best friend.

My person.

13

Cleocatra

It was nice hearing Dad's voice last night.

Of course he was the one to remember the treats.

He always remembers.

I know he's trying to apologize for letting my human take me on this trip. She's lucky I like car rides, or this could be a lot worse.

For now, he's forgiven.

The treats having catnip in them—unbeknownst to her—helped.

She'll regret this in the middle of the night when I can't sleep.

But I'll be too high-strung to care.

14

PAIGE

Dear Rhodes,

The mutant bees forced me inside all night, but that meant we got to talk.

I told you this on the phone, but I miss you. More than I thought I would. I'm happy to be on this journey; I really am. It's pushed me to learn things I wouldn't have otherwise and required a level of alone time I've also never had.

Like now, alone in my thoughts.

It's a weird feeling since I don't have a boyfriend to call—someone else to think or worry about. Even my parents and Constance are being abnormally quiet today. The Wi-Fi at this campground is also spotty, making it impossible to rewatch all of my favorite shows, and I can't even sit outside because *bees*.

But I have a new resolve after our call tonight. I'm going to do this. I'll see it through, and when I tell you I love you back, I'll be ready for everything you have to give.

And that isn't as scary as I thought it would be to admit.

Yours,
Paige

15

Paige

"Hey, Siri, how do you change a flat tire?"

"Playing How to Change a Tire by—"

"That's not what I meant!" I press the "X" on my phone screen before she can finish.

She doesn't seem ruffled like I am. "I'm sorry, I didn't catch that."

I groan loudly, throwing my head back to look at the sky. At least it's blue and not sporting any rain clouds like it probably would if I were still in Washington. But the weather still never cooperates when you need it to since the sun is nearly at its highest point in the day and threatening to burn my skin.

It's a good thing I lathered myself in sunscreen this morning when leaving the bee-infested campground. I left with only one sting on my palm while swatting at the little vermin. It's currently wrapped in gauze I found in the first aid kit Mom packed for me. She didn't approve of the three Band-Aids and medical scissors I packed myself. The scissors were actually not going to be used for anything medical at all. They're just the only scissors I own.

Worse than a bum hand was that I got so close to calling Rhodes to help me with this ten minutes ago when it happened. I almost had to swat the phone out of my hand so I wouldn't. But that would be no help to anyone.

I was frazzled by all of the road noise and seeing the absolute shit state my back right tire was in after it decided to burst like a balloon with fresh helium inside. Plus, I know for a fact he's changed a flat tire before because his dad has always been really into survivalist-type stuff and put him through a series of tests. Changing a tire was one of the things among knotting and plant identification.

It might be the reason Rhodes likes to eat plants so much.

That makes so much sense now.

But after the initial freak out and pacing along the busy road, I told myself I could figure this out. I *would* figure it out.

By. My. Self.

It's just another test in learning how to be okay on my own.

I'm going to change the fuck out of this tire.

Except it's barely recognizable now. The tire is in tatters, and I rode the wheel rim to the side of the road where traffic now rushes past at a terrifying speed, making it too loud to hear much—in Siri's defense.

But I can't just do nothing.

Pulling up a new internet tab, I type out *how to change a tire like a badass*

Then finally, *finally*, a list of video links pops up on my screen, instilling my hope in technology once again. The small robot that lives inside my phone came through.

I click the first link and the man in the video immediately starts talking and telling me to take a deep breath because it will all be okay. He will help me. The man has a beard and flannel, making him look ten times more knowledgeable. But he starts using names like *jack* and *crank* without much explanation. I'll need a video breakdown of his video just to understand.

Skip.

The next one is a woman, and I instantly like her. She holds up what I now know is a tool called a *jack* and not some random man who will appear out of thin air to help change my tire.

Unfortunate, if you ask me.

I've never changed a tire before but now seems like the perfect opportunity to figure out how. I refuse to call anyone and end up back where I started. The bird incident wasn't so bad.

Scratch that.

It was.

But I've managed without my parents *or* Rhodes so far.

I can do this, too.

I pause the video and rummage through the back of my van, shoving aside a pool noodle, an oar, and a tire pump for the bike I didn't bring before finding Jack. Or *the* jack, but I'm attached to this being his name now. He's a heavy chunk of metal painted yellow and has one arm, but it's apparently a very strong arm that will lift the weight of Vincent VanGo who looks like he's hit the unleaded gas a few too many times in his life.

I press play and follow each step Cynthia tells me to do.

So far, she is way better than Siri.

And Lumberjack Jesus.

While I situate Jack the right way, I realize I can only hear every other word Cynthia says. So, I switch to headphones hanging out in the front cupholder, prop my phone on Jack, and start pumping.

Sweat beads on my forehead, and I silently—okay, not so silently—curse my biceps, triceps, and all the other *ceps* in my body for being so small. Rhodes could probably break Jack with those burly forearms of his.

Don't do that! I internally chide. *Don't you dare think about his forearms at a time like this*!

Cynthia continues her very passionate speech about lug nuts, which includes a fairly extensive history lesson on artillery wheels where the tire was actually bolted directly to the wheel, making a flat tire change quite challenging.

The more you know.

Her thorough explanation and positive demeanor are helpful despite having to pause and play key parts multiple times over until I finally get the destroyed tire off and the spare on. It was a feat to wrestle it out of the small compartment in my trunk, under my bed, and beneath all of my things. I had to remove bins of underwear, socks, and random items I lovingly refer to as my *junk drawer*.

It was worth it, though, because I'm staring at the rear of my van with new appreciation. A kind of reverence and awe I haven't felt before.

The spare tire might as well be shiny and made of gold; it's so perfect.

I check the lug nuts once more to make sure they are properly tightened before loading my van back up. There's a spring in my step even with the very present sweat on my brow and dirt smudges all across my fair skin. But I'm proud of every smear, including the ones on my white tank.

It's a reminder that *I did this.*

"I did this," I say out loud, hands on my hips, just to confirm it really happened. "I did this!"

The way I can't help but fist-punch the air and let out a little scream like a wild animal who just got their first kill.

I'm elated.

I survived a flat tire.

My first one.

Test complete.

16

RHODES

"Paige?" I'm pretty sure I mumble.

"Rhodes! I did it."

I blink several times, and I lift my head off my pillow, trying to register what she's saying and where her voice is coming from. It sounds far off, with background noise competing to be heard.

My neck releases and my head flops back on the pillow.

"Rhodes!" she yells again.

I smile, thinking I have to be dreaming. "Yes, Paige? Are you back for more?"

"Back for more?" she repeats. "What are you talking about? Wake up! I have to tell you something."

In my dream, I imagine Paige is in the kitchen, which I can't quite see from my bed while lying flat on my back. She's telling me we should have ice cream, and I should lick it off her.

No, that's not right.

Why am I holding my phone?

I blink several times again, peering into the kitchen to see that Paige is *not* naked in the kitchen with ice cream and instead calling my name through the device in my hand. "Paige?"

"Yes! Are you awake, or do you still think you're dreaming?"

Propping to my elbow, I scrub my other hand down my face. "I'm awake." I think. "Did you call me, or did I somehow call you?"

I must have fallen asleep after my midafternoon pickleball practice...with myself. Amber couldn't make it, which makes sense since I'm the only one keeping a rigorous two-hour per-day schedule.

"Yes! I couldn't wait to tell you," she says again. "I left the bee campground for Missoula with Cleo, who was up all night running around the van thanks to your treats..." She takes a breath. "Never mind. That's beside the point. What I'm trying to say is that I had a flat tire and changed it on my own. I did it! I could probably change another one right now. I mean, with Cynthia's help, but still. I could do it if I had to, and I DID!"

"Cynthia?"

"Oh!" she yells through the line. "She's my new favorite DIY-er. I only scanned her other videos, but she has everything from art projects using plastic bags to how-to's on just about anything home or auto-related with random history facts for fun."

There's so much pride in her voice; it's contagious. "Wow, you did it," I say almost wistfully.

Not that I didn't think she could, just that I know this feeling. When you try something hard and end up seeing the other side.

"I did it!"

"I'm really proud of you. Where are you now?"

"I have no idea!" she yells through what sounds like pure adrenaline. "I'm somewhere in Idaho going very slowly on the freeway. I changed the tire, but it's not like I could exactly test that it was on properly without driving, so I'm pissing a lot of people off, but that's okay because I DID IT!"

"You did it." I smile and push myself to a seated position on my bed. "Have you called anyone else?"

"Just you," she confirms.

Just you.

My entire body comes to life like I hadn't been fast asleep seconds ago.

She laughs. "I'm sure Mom will want to put this in my baby book or something."

She's probably right about that one. "I hope you took a photo."

"At least twenty," she says. "There was no way I wanted to forget this. I'll likely tell my grandchildren about it."

I scrub a hand down my face, unable to keep myself from smiling at the prospect. "I hope I'm there to witness it."

"You will be."

I appreciate her spirit. "So where are you headed now?"

"I found a small town about an hour away from me that has a tire shop. But based on my current speed, I'll probably get there kind of late. I need to stop for gas soon, too."

"Hey," I say, catching her attention.

"What?"

"You did it."

"I did it," she says like she's ready to burst into song and dance. "Rhodes?"

I brace a hand behind my head and lean against the headboard. "Yeah?"

"Thank you for answering so I could share. I wanted to call you earlier so badly, but I needed to prove to myself I could do it more." She pauses. "And I guess I can say I know how to change a tire now."

I smile at this. "A skill you didn't have until today."

She laughs. "I know you've basically taken a crash course in all things car related and could probably change Cassandra's footwear with your eyes closed."

Cassandra is the name I gave my car to appease Paige's prodding that it needed one. "You're probably right, but look at what you did; you didn't need me."

This doesn't cause me to break out in a nervous sweat like it might have a couple days ago. Instead, I'm smiling when I say it.

"Are you okay, though? Still have all your fingers?" Some things won't change, like needing to know she's safe after an ordeal such as this one.

"Besides a few bruises I'm sure I'll find tomorrow, everything is accounted for," she says before exhaling long and slow. "Thank you for celebrating with me."

"Always," I say in a whisper.

After hanging up with Paige, I get out of bed and pad into the kitchen, bare-footed and ready to eat. I hadn't planned on falling asleep for so long, but it's almost three, and I haven't eaten since breakfast.

I ran through multiple scenarios Jim and Agnes might want to use in our upcoming game, visualizing myself taking them down. I guess it wore me out.

But as I pull out some things to make sandwiches, I feel weird.

Why do I feel this way?

Paige was so excited to have changed the tire on her own, and what I said was true: I am proud of her. But maybe I just feel weird because my reaction is so different than I expected. I was missing a few words in this conversation compared to the one after the bird incident that are better left unsaid.

The control freak in me took a backseat to let the easygoing, you-go-girl part of me shine.

This is exactly what she wanted from this trip, and I suppose it's what I needed, too, in order to confirm I'd be alright. When Dad's stroke forced him into months of physical therapy, Mom and I were completely powerless. I didn't like that feeling. Still don't. But I'm surprised to find that this—Paige stepping out on her own—isn't that.

I've always been the go-getter, control-everything-in-my-life type.

The kind of person who may not know the answer but can figure it out. And with Paige, it's always been easy to swoop in and be the firm rock for her to lean on. I like it that way. It's a role I know how to be in.

But that's not how love works.

It's slippery and wild and a little unruly.

I want to protect her, be with her, tell her how much I love her, but that's not what love is asking of me right now, and it's weird. Love is asking me to cheer her on, clap loudly, and maybe get a poster board with some obnoxiously positive saying on it to wave around.

I slather a heap of chipotle mayo on two slices of sourdough, loading it with turkey, cheese, alfalfa sprouts, cucumbers, and tomatoes and thinking about how, if Paige were here, she'd ask for a PB&J instead.

It makes me smile to think about.

Being here, front and center, simply for the experience of watching her change before my eyes is worth it. I'm trusting the process even if it goes against everything in me, and finding that it isn't that bad.

This is letting go, and so far, it doesn't feel like I'm dying.

17

Paige

Dear Rhodes,

I know I already told you this, but I'm at a gas station and wanted to tell you again.

I did it.

That is all.

Yours,
Paige

18

Paige

Staying in this small town isn't what I had in mind.

I should be lighting a fire and sitting in my cozy chair with a glass of wine in one hand and my book in another while at the bougie campground I booked in Missoula to celebrate the fact I made it that far.

Goodbye complimentary outdoor gas fireplace and golf cart.

Instead, I found a campground in Wallace, Idaho, on the outskirts of town with a coin-operated shower and a babbling creek through the middle of it—emphasis on the *babble*. It's small and peaceful and better than a grocery store parking lot, which was my second option.

After the tire debacle, I stopped here to get it fixed, only to realize they were already closed...two minutes before I arrived. The man closing up shop told me he had to leave for his kid's soccer game and couldn't stay, but he'd get to me first thing in the morning.

With it starting to get dark out, I decided to stay the night, canceling tonight's reservation in Missoula for...nature. And lots of it since this campground is tucked into the side of the mountain. I'll still get to stay at the bougie place tomorrow night, but for now, this one will have to do.

I'm starving, and after my day, I'm ready for anywhere that sells beer.

I never drink beer, but tonight, I do.

The benefit of my lodging is everything is within walking distance. So, I grabbed my purse and headed into the center of the tree-lined streets. There are quite a few restaurants here in the middle of the mountains, with the freeway overpass going directly over a portion of this tiny town.

A pub on the corner looks promising with its doors swung wide, music and booming laughter drifting out into the night air. There's a touch of chill tonight thanks to the peaks surrounding us, blocking the last bits of the sun's warmth. Who knew this place even existed with its cute shops, single grocery store, and four-way stops in lieu of stoplights?

I almost didn't believe there was a mechanic shop here when I looked it up on my phone map. The mountains turned into more mountains the further I drove, winding and dipping enough to force my eyes to stay on the road at all times.

I gave Cleo her food before talking to the man at the shop earlier, along with a few treats—courtesy of her second favorite person. She'll be fine for a while. And I will be, too, once I get a beer and some food. The adrenaline has worn off, and I feel a little like a limp noodle.

Walking inside, there's a hostess stand, which really seems like more of a suggestion since the couple who enters behind me passes straight by it to head for the bar. So, I follow them as if we're all together in case I get in trouble for seating myself. There are quite a few people in here for it being seven o'clock on a Wednesday, but I'm able to find a spot further down the bar.

It isn't as loud now that I'm in here. The music plays at a reasonable volume, and the ambiance is unique, with oil cans as lampshades hanging above the bartop and a wall of mirrors behind the liquor bottles. Luckily, everyone here is dressed casually. I don't think I stand out too much in my jean shorts, tank top with dainty flowers on it, and dirt smudges on my arms and legs from changing my tire.

I take that back.

They aren't *this* casual.

My bare legs stick to the red leather barstools as I look through the menu. The woman behind the bar approaches with water and a smile. "You visiting?"

I drop the menu with a thwack and sigh, looking every bit as exhausted as I feel, I'm sure. "Is it really obvious?"

Her hair is a deep, auburn color with strands of gray sprinkled throughout and caught in two braids hanging past her shoulders. Her T-shirt and jeans give her a *normal* vibe, making her instantly likable. That and the small but friendly smile she wears.

She scratches her cheek. "You've got a smudge."

I lift my hand to wipe at the spot on my face. "Of course I do." Snagging a napkin, I dip it in my water and wipe my entire cheek, hoping I'll get it. She doesn't seem to mind my lack of manners. I'm sure working at a bar means she's seen worse. "I had a flat tire and had to change it on the interstate. I've never done it before, so it took a couple of hours. I'm starving and need a beer. Whatever you suggest."

I smile in case my exhaustion makes me sound rude.

She nods, hand splayed wide while propped on the bar's edge. "I'll bring two drinks."

"I only need one."

"Oh. No," she says and points at the draft beers. "I'm getting one for you *and* me. It's my break. I'll bring some of the chicken wings, too. Figure you've got a story to tell and need an ear to listen."

I guess it would be nice to talk to someone. Cleo sure got an earful on the drive here; I bet she's glad to get a break and leave the listening to someone else.

"I'm Nelly." She slides an ice-cold beer across the bartop minutes later. "It's local. Not too bad."

"Paige." We clink glasses, then I chug half of mine, dribbling a little down my chin.

She smiles behind the rim of her frosted glass cup. "Where you from?"

"Tacoma, Washington."

"Where ya headed?"

"Montana, then Yellowstone."

She nods. "Lots of folks like you heading to the park this time of year. I meet a few every day."

"Really?"

She nods and sets her beer down in front of her, gripping the edges of the counter. "Everyone wants a piece of that national park in some way or another."

"It's my first time," I say, painting smooth lines along the side of my glass. "I'm on a...journey."

It still sounds ridiculous to say it out loud, but I don't stop there. Nope. Instead, I give her all the gory details, including the descriptive and far too spicy dream I had about Rhodes, the kiss we shared in the parking lot, and The Itch that won't go away.

Cue me offering far too much information, per usual.

She said she wanted to listen.

"The further I get, the more I think this trip was just meant for me to find out what I want to do with my life," I explain. "And I want to figure myself out, too, because Rhodes is the best man I've ever known. He has his own place, a job he's passionate about, a 401k, and a sizable savings account. I have a cat."

"So, what do you want to do with your life?" Nelly asks, sipping her brew.

I furrow my brows, concentrating on a large knick in the glossy wood in front of me. "Well, I should probably decide on a career. I've changed jobs too many times to count."

"What kind of jobs?"

I tick them off on my finger. "Tupperware sales, pet psychic hotline, too many craft businesses to name individually, and most recently, working at Upstairs Closet Thrift."

"And you didn't like any of those?"

I shrug. "Not enough to continue working there forever."

Except for Upstairs Closet Thrift, which was the first job that actually felt like it was a good fit. My schedule was flexible, often changing week to week, and the days were always different. Whether I was sorting and working the floor, rotating new inventory, and experiencing peculiar personalities who came through the doors were always entertaining. I loved it.

Maybe quitting was a rash decision. But my old boss, Don, had to go and inspire me to take some time to be on my own and decide what I really wanted.

So, I did that.

To the extreme, but still.

She waves me off and stands straighter. "Okay, someone has to tell you."

"Tell me what?" I cradle my beer glass, looking on and waiting.

"Do you know how many jobs I've had over the years? I'm sixty."

Sixty? I wouldn't have guessed.

I shake my head and throw out a guess. "Seven?"

"Twenty-three." Her piercing gaze is serious and unwavering. "Jobs come and go. They change like the weather. You can't tie your self-worth to a job." She points at her chest roughly. "You have to find that inside yourself."

I can't hold her stare any longer and peer down at my near-empty glass. There's an understanding inside me that says she's right, even if I'm still trying to sort that out in my head.

"So, what makes *you* happy?"

I blow a stray strand of hair out of my face. "Men," I answer honestly. "Men make me happy."

"Honey, there isn't a man who can do as good a job as you when it comes to happiness." She levels a knowing glare at me. "Come on, now. What are some things you love? The things you spend your time thinking about, and the ones that excite you?"

I wasn't lying when I said men, though I'm starting to realize maybe this is one of my problems. Getting tied up in someone else makes it difficult to let myself shine.

"Um..." I bounce my knee. "I love to sew, animals, interior design..."

"Now take your skills and what you love and do more of those. It doesn't need to be complicated." Before I can answer, she pushes off the bar suddenly. "Break's over, and it looks like we've got a few new customers."

I peer toward the entrance to see a large group coming through, rowdy and yelling in jest over the music.

"Wash up over there," Nelly points at a sink near the kitchen doors, "and come help me."

I stare blankly at her. "What?"

"Do you see anyone else around here?" She waves behind the bar area, and she's right; no one else is there.

When she said she was taking a break, I assumed there would be someone to cover for her. Guess not.

I blink rapidly a few more beats, then determine she isn't screwing with me. I stand and round the bar to do exactly as she says, even though I've never mixed a drink before in my life.

"YOU'RE A NATURAL."

"I don't know about that." I pull the draft lever, tipping the glass enough to avoid getting too much foam while also getting a good pour, just like Nelly said to do.

We've been at this for at least an hour, but I've honestly lost track of time, and this bar doesn't have a clock anywhere. The rowdy group eventually left when Nelly told them to walk home and go to bed. They complained, but only for a short spell since she threatened to call their wives and families to pick them up. That got them out the doors and walking real fast.

I slide the beer across the bartop to an older gentleman and wipe my hands on a towel while Nelly leans her forearms beside me. "You jumped in without any notice and figured things out. I barely had to tell you what to do."

"It helps that no one ordered anything complicated. Beer, wine, and whiskey on the rocks are easy to handle."

Nelly squints at me. "You don't give yourself enough credit. Not everyone can do that. You're pretty flexible, you know. That's a hard skill to teach just anyone."

I drop the towel and lean my hip against the bar to face her. "Was this all part of your lesson to show me I've got something to offer and I'm not a washed-up thirty-year-old?"

She leans into one elbow and shrugs. "Did it work?"

The corner of my mouth lifting gives me away. "Maybe. I guess I am pretty flexible. I really enjoyed this tonight. I felt…useful."

"Well, you aren't useless just because you're not doing what you love right now. Just remember it's important to enjoy your job, too." She twirls a finger. "Why do you think I work here? I like the people, the conversations, and being a forward-facing part of the community."

I nod and meet her eyes. "I guess I was worried the thrift store wasn't a *grown-up* job, and maybe I couldn't settle down because I'm not really a grown-up. I barely made enough to afford rent."

"Fair. But the secret to being a grown-up," she says, "is realizing you don't need anything external to fulfill you, but maybe you want it. Even the billionaires aren't immune from unhappiness."

There aren't a lot of times I've found myself in a bar on a random Wednesday, talking to a woman my mother's age, who has completely upended what I thought. But this wouldn't have been possible unless I said *fuck it* and left my bubble.

"I think I get it," I say. "So I just have to figure out how to be fulfilled inside myself and then go after what I want."

"Yes." She nods once.

I stand straighter, looking around the bar with renewed vigor, until I realize one more thing. A BIG thing. One that feels critical to actually being able to understand this new concept.

"How do I do that?"

19

CLEOCATRA

My dish is empty.

I'm trying not to take this as a personal offense, but it's hard not to.

If only I were trusted outside to hunt.

I swear I could do it.

I've killed birds, a few mice, but they are always immediately taken from me—an insult to the highest degree.

I don't even have the pleasure of batting them around a little.

And now Nature is *right there*.

In fact, there's a fat Magpie sitting on a low branch directly in my line of sight. I swear it's saying my name, provoking me to *do* something.

I wish I could, little fucker.

You'd be dead before you could make that annoying sound again.

Soon enough I will get my revenge.

Soon enough.

20

PAIGE

Spend time alone with yourself.

I can check off Nelly's advice for how to feel fulfilled since I'm currently holed up in my van while rain pelts the fiberglass roof.

I've spent most of this trip inside this van rather than exploring outside.

So much for enjoying the bougie campground.

After getting my tire fixed early this morning, I swung back by the bar for some food since Nelly assured me she'd be working, and breakfast at a bar isn't all that weird in a small town. She even made me a pecan latte to go along with my sausage and egg sandwich, which I scarfed down, managing to save a few bites of the meat pattie for Cleo as a treat.

By the time I got to Missoula, the clouds had rolled in, heavy with rain, which let loose the moment I checked in and pulled into the nicely paved spot I booked for far too much money a night.

The pool and hot tub they highlighted on their social media were a siren call.

Too bad, since the rain has put a huge damper on reading my book poolside. With rain pelting my roof in a beat that sounds a whole lot like a sped-up version of "We Will Rock You," I'm staring at all of the eyes on my wall, thinking about how Rhodes said it would feel like they're looking at me. I heartily disagreed, but now I see what he was saying. The eyes aren't judgmental, but they are watchful. Watching to see if I'm going to figure out how to be alone and observing how much I suck at it.

I can't take it anymore.

I turn my back on them, facing the double doors I hoped to be able to open up and watch the sunrise or sunset from the comfort of my bed like all of the van influencers do. But not me.

I'm dealing with bees and rain.

Picking up my phone off the charger, I text Amber.

Me:
I'm regretting the eyes.

There. I said it.

The wind whistles outside while I wait for her reply.

Amber:
Are you telling me so you don't have to admit Rhodes was right?

Me:
Maybe.

Me:
Okay, yes.

Me:
But they are starting to creep me out.

Amber:
LOL

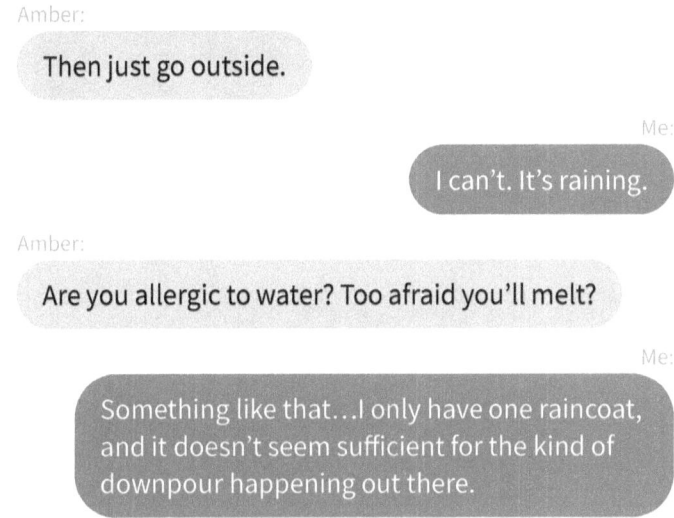

I stare at the coat hanging on a Command hook right behind the driver's seat. Living in Washington, where it rains a lot, doesn't mean I own proper gear. It's kind of a mark of pride *not* to use an umbrella. But Montana rain isn't drizzly by any means. It's a full-on downpour that has me questioning whether my van will be picked up and carried downstream.

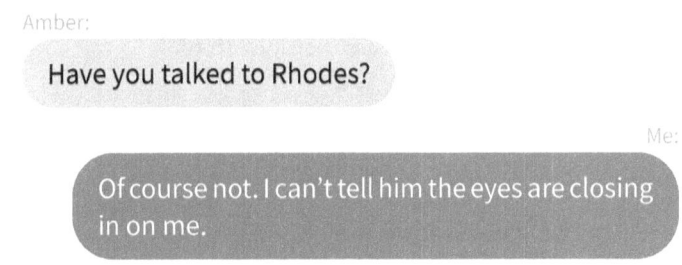

He'd just love that.

Rhodes isn't one to gloat, but I imagine him doing it, and it's enough to make me keep some thoughts to myself.

Amber:
> No, I meant about…other things.

Did Rhodes tell Amber that I like him?

> **Me:** What other things?

> **Amber:** Pickleball…

I laugh to myself and lay back on my bed. It bounces Cleo slightly, and she looks at me as though I've never done worse. A quick scratch on her ears and all is forgiven, though.

> **Me:** He told me he picked it up so he could stop thinking about me.

Or that I was gone, but I can read between the lines. Sometimes.

> **Amber:** I'm surprised he said that much.

> **Me:** Yeah, well, I sort of…like him. And knowing he's trying to give me space to have this trip is sweet.

It feels odd to type it out rather than just think it in my head, but Amber is my best friend and knows how much I've struggled the last few weeks.

> **Amber:** Of course you like him. That much was obvious. I'm waiting to find out what you're planning to do about it.

> **Me:** I'm going to figure out how to be alone with myself, be honest about how I'm feeling, and eat a lot of tacos.

Amber: So...you're going to do nothing about your feelings then?

I let out a slow breath.

Me: I guess so. For now.

Amber: Who are you?

Me: I barely know. But he was convinced I needed time, and I think he's right. I'm always jumping from one relationship to the next for all the wrong reasons. This time, I want to do it for the right ones.

Amber: And what are the right ones?

I think about what Nelly said at her bar last night.

Me: That I want to be with Rhodes because we add to each other's lives instead of needing him to fulfill something inside me.

Amber: Now I really don't recognize you.

Amber: But you know Rhodes is as faithful as ever. He'll give you the time you need.

> Me:
> That's what I'm afraid of. How much time is the right amount of time? I don't want to rush things like I did with the other guys.

> Amber:
> I see Rhodes as being in a completely different category than "other guys." He's been your best friend for as long almost as I have. He knows you, and you know him. Just figure out what you need and then tell him. Don't make him suffer.

> Amber:
> Selfishly, I can only handle so much exercise.

I laugh and send her a middle finger emoji, then sit up and stare at my raincoat again.

I'm going to do it.

I'm going to go outside.

MY SNEAKERS ARE less than ideal to be trudging through muddy grass, but I'm determined not to let a little rain squander my time here.

Russell Crow almost convinced me to go home.

The bees already tried to destroy me.

My flat tire wanted me to cry.

Not the rain, too.

I have to keep my eyes on the ground to watch where I step since the earth is soft and sludgy, ready to absorb my feet as though it were really quicksand.

But I keep going. There's a trail leading up a short embankment that looks made of gravel and is much easier to walk on, so I set my eyes on it. The woman at the front desk assured me this path circles the entire park. I've already passed three pools, one with a water slide and spray park that is currently closed, and a playground I would have died to play on as a kid. Honestly, I still might if it doesn't rain tomorrow.

Then my phone begins to ring.

I pull it out and see Constance's name scrawled on it, answering immediately.

"Are Mom and Dad okay?"

"Yes," she states, void of emotion. "Why wouldn't they be?"

Because she's calling me for the first time since I left. "No reason. What's up?"

"I need to borrow your room."

"You mean my basement apartment?"

She isn't amused. "I mean the basement room you lived in."

"*Live* in," I correct. "You know I'm coming back?"

Silence ensues once I reach the small hill leading to the path. It's bigger than I thought, with dispersed trees and rocks, making it look like a game to walk up.

"Yes, I know you're coming back. But in like a year."

"I said *weeks*, Constance."

"You said you had to find yourself."

I push the hood of my rain jacket out of my face as it tries to blind me while I climb. "That's right."

"Two weeks won't be enough time for that. A year, minimum."

"I appreciate the confidence," I grunt, pitching forward, nearly on my hands and knees as I climb. "What do you even need the space for?"

"Stuff."

I slip, my knee sinking into mud. "What kind of stuff?"

"A business thing."

"Constance!" I grind out, trying to brush off chunks of mud from my jeans. "I don't have the patience for this right now. Just tell me!"

"A grow operation, okay!" she shouts back.

I pause, standing straighter and breathing heavily. "Like weed?"

"Don't be ridiculous," she states in a condescending tone. "I need to turn the basement into a greenhouse so I can sell house plants."

My patience is thinner than my coat right now, which is saying a lot since I can already feel rain seeping through the supposed waterproof layer. I stare at the remaining hillside left to climb and say on an exhale that forces my shoulders to slump, "No."

She hangs up quickly, and I pocket my phone so I have both hands to grab onto trees and climb. This isn't the first time she's asked for some weird request, but I haven't been in this circumstance when she's asked. I manage to make it to the top with mud on my knees, hands, and my face by the tight feel of it.

But I keep going.

Despite the rain, birds are calling to each other from one branch perch to another, chirping as though they have something important to say. The tree branches lining the one-lane trail, wide enough for a car to pass, sway slightly with the light gusts that blow through at random intervals, and I have to dodge the greedy puddles absorbing every raindrop that falls.

The air smells clean and fresh, while my runny nose tells me it's cold outside.

This feels like another test. Another way I'm learning how to be on my—

My phone rings again, and I wrestle it from my pocket.

"Hi, Mom—"

"Honey, where's the bundt cake pan I like to use?" she starts in. "I can't find it anywhere."

Really?

"No idea, Mom. Have you asked Constance?"

"You know she doesn't bake."

Baking to Constance is akin to torture, but mostly because she doesn't like getting her hands messy. To be fair, when Mom and I bake, we somehow are covered head-to-toe in flour. Constance's all-black wardrobe wouldn't mix well with this.

"What about Dad?"

"He's getting the car serviced."

"Okay, well, I'm on a hike and totally useless right now."

She sighs. "I'll just find something else. Thanks, sweetie."

She hangs up, and I slide my phone back into my pocket. It would be great if I could actually pass this test of being alone without my family calling every three seconds.

I've always loved how close we are. Even with Constance in our own way. But breaking away and separating myself from the family has come with its challenges. I can't help but feel I'm always missing out on something. Mom told me just yesterday how she got a haircut...three days ago. How could she not tell me?

But then there's this other part of me that deliberately pulled away, needing the practice of flying out of the nest instead of falling like it feels I've been doing for years. I don't want to miss out on their lives, but I also don't want to stay nest-bound for the entirety of mine.

Boundaries aren't a bad thing, I don't think. I've just never been good at setting them.

You know what?

I pull my phone out and turn it to silent. I've never done this before, too worried someone would need me or there would be an emergency I could miss—like a haircut. But so far, nothing has been important enough to disrupt this peace.

Surprisingly, I feel a little more free, maybe even a touch reckless, for silencing my phone.

It's just me, nature, and—

My foot lands with a splash in a large puddle, soaking my jeans to the muddy knee. At first, my mouth hangs open, hands splayed wide since droplets of water sprang up all the way to my face. My glasses are already fogged up thanks to the moisture in the air, making it difficult to see. I slowly drop my arms to my side, and I do something that feels out of character for this moment.

I smile.

Like a real one that I can feel stretching my lips to their furthest capacity, then I do the unthinkable.

I laugh.

A giggle at the back of my throat to start, and then an audible one that forces my chest to rattle. It reminds me of Winnie after Cleo tried to dig up the dead bird we'd just buried, but it's also more than that. It's the feeling I had knowing Penny could help me become better acquainted with my rig, or I could change a tire on my own. When I helped Nelly serve behind the bar or the second I kissed Rhodes in the parking lot, and I forgot about the before and wasn't worried about the after—just the moment.

It's quiet, apart from my laughter cutting through the rain.

Cold but still warm enough to create moisture in the air.

I'm alone but not lonely.

It's a freeing thought, really, to *not* be accessible.

To be drenched and laughing and *okay*.

Looking up at the sky, I let the raindrops batter my glasses and dribble down my

cheeks, some even sliding down my neck beneath my jacket, causing me to shiver. For the first time in as long as I can remember, I feel good.

Okay enough to be here in this moment and not feel like I need to move on to the next. And certainly okay enough not to need to reach for my phone and call someone. I'm just here, feeling each raindrop, losing track while trying to count them, and being comfortable in my skin despite the conditions. I've spent a lot of my life being there for other people, but at this moment, I am simply here for me—laughing and maybe crying a little because I understand what adventure really is.

It's people and places, the known and the unknown.

It's trying something new.

It's failing.

It's anything but linear.

For the first time in a while, The Itch isn't there, nagging at the back of my mind.

And I think I'm going to be okay.

21

PAIGE

Dear Rhodes,

I just realized something.

I think I like being by myself.

I never used to. Being alone meant I was failing somehow. When the person I was dating eventually left, it meant I did something wrong that made them leave. I couldn't make them stay. I couldn't change myself, adapt, and shift my priorities enough to make them stay with me. I hated that feeling.

But this feeling?

The one where I can visualize what it looks like to actually be okay and fly instead of fall for once…it feels like a big deal.

I get it now. Or, at least, I'm starting to.

Yours,
Paige

22

RHODES

"All we have to do is hold them and score more," I explain to Amber in our huddle.

"Isn't that the point of all sports?"

I stare past her shoulder at the sixty-year-old duo stretching out their quads. "Yes, but it's true for right now, too."

We're nearing the end of the game, and we aren't that far behind. Amber's backhand is looking miles better than it did earlier this week, and all of the strategies I've learned online are really helping.

"I think we can win." I've been hesitant to say this out loud because I didn't want to jinx anything.

I'm wearing my lucky socks with avocados, so I'm probably safe.

"They're still too good."

I shush her. "Don't say that! They are good, but we've also made them work for every point. I'm going to keep the pressure on them from the back, and you take them to the net."

"What the hell does that mean?" Amber says, hands on her knees as she catches her breath.

I arch a brow. "Take them to the net?"

She nods.

Jim and Agnes are looking smug for two people about to lose. "It means *end them*."

Amber smirks while continuing to nod. "Yeah, yeah. I like that."

I didn't think I was competitive, but participating in a blind dating experiment with two other guys vying for the love of my life really did a number on me. It unlocked something.

I'm not leaving here without a win.

"Destroy them on three," Amber says, throwing her hand between us. I set mine on hers, and she starts counting. "One, two, three...destroy them!"

She said the last part louder than I expected her to, but it's worth the surprise in Jim and Agnes' eyes.

I lower my gaze at them, pointing from me to them, not entirely sure what I'm communicating. But Jim locks his jaw and throws up a couple of fingers to point between my eyes and his.

He's watching me.

Well, I'm watching him.

Amber takes her spot closer to the net, and I hold up the lightweight ball, raising my paddle with the other hand.

I hit the ball hard, and it soars over Amber's head to the other side of the net like a gazelle leaping over a wall.

Destroy them.

"THEY DESTROYED US." Amber swivels her head to look at me.

I'm leaning forward while sitting, head in my hands. The end of that game did not go as planned. Apparently, Jim had another setting he unlocked, and Agnes was hiding the fact her new knees were better than the old ones.

"We'll get them next time."

"Next time?" Amber says with a high-pitched tone.

I sit back on the bench, leaning against the glass wall like she is. Her arms are crossed, brows bent in a harsh angle—down, not up. "You heard them." I gesture toward the now-empty court. Nearly everyone in the gym flanked the sidelines while watching us a half hour ago. "They want to play us again."

Amber kicks her volume up a notch. "Yeah, so they can murder us!"

"It wasn't that bad," I say, blowing her off.

It definitely was.

And while I'm bummed about our loss, I know I did my best. I'm proud, even, maybe a little happy because I really enjoyed myself.

She scoffs and huffs like she's out of words but not feelings.

Maybe things would have gone differently if I'd practiced more, watched more game plan strategies, or had a partner who didn't need to lay down in the middle of a serve. But no, we were thoroughly beaten, and it only gives me more steam to do better next time.

My phone rings with a video call, and the photo Paige sent me last night lights up the screen.

She should be at the Bozeman Hot Springs campground after her one-night stays in Wallace and then Missoula, which was completely soaked by rain, according to my weather app. But the photo of her with trees taller than her and mountains taller than them in the background indicated she was doing just fine.

Better than fine.

Beautiful, breathtaking, and so full of life.

I made the picture my phone's wallpaper, and her contact photo, so I could stare at it anytime I wanted.

Amber chugs more of her water, and with the echoed silence of this court, I answer with, "Happy almost birthday!"

"Hi! Rhodes!"

I've stopped actively sweating since the game ended, but I'm sure I still look like it took a toll on me. It's nothing like her.

She isn't exactly in a position I expected to see her in on a Saturday morning. The slim straps of her orange bikini tie around her neck, the triangles covering her acting like cautionary arrows. I shouldn't stare, but I do.

"Paige," I say. The ache in my chest starts to pound, and the blood circulating through my body is now directed to one place. I use the towel to drape over my lap. "How are you?"

"I made it to the hot springs!" she says. "It's so nice here. I pulled in and came directly here to soak. I'm basically a prune now." She lifts one hand to the screen to show me the ripples on her fingers.

"I see that." Is it just me, or do I sound like a robot?

"What is wrong with you? She's in a bikini, not lingerie," Amber says, snatching the phone.

"Paige, hi, happy almost birthday. And yeah, we lost our game, Rhodes thinks you're hot, and based on the suspicious placement of his towel, I'm guessing he's going to be thinking about this image all night."

Paige laughs while I glare at Amber with a look that could split a hair in half with my mind. She doesn't seem to care one iota.

I snatch my phone back, glaring at her until I'm looking at Paige again. My expression melts into one of total adoration. She *is* hot. And I want nothing more than to tell her that right now.

"I'm sorry you guys lost," she says, propping her phone against something in order to redo her hair.

It rests just above her shoulders when down, but she gathers it all into a small ponytail with flyaways and pieces still hanging at the nape of her neck. All I can focus on is how her bicep muscles contract while raised above her head. The lift of her breasts in that perfect swimsuit made just for her, like a second skin that isn't even necessary.

"You're perfect," I find myself thinking.

Actually, I don't just think it.

I must have said it out loud because Amber's cruel snickering in the background clues me in.

I close my mouth, though it doesn't seem like she heard me, as Paige dips below the water to wet her shoulders before standing to her full height. She might be short, but the angle...

I turn to Amber and whisper, "You need to leave."

She laughs. "Not a chance. My legs don't work anymore, remember?"

"Fine," I say, standing and grabbing my few items while clutching the small towel to my groin. "I'll leave." Directing my attention back to Paige, I tell her, "Hold on, I'm heading to the locker room."

"Bye, Amber! I'll call you later," Paige yells.

"Call me and tell me your plans to celebrate!" Amber calls back. "And check your email to find your present."

I tip my chin at Amber in goodbye and push through the glass double doors before quickly making my way down the carpeted hallway toward the locker rooms. I'm inside, dumping my things and scanning for others. No one else is here right now, which I can thank Jim and Agnes for—something I never thought I'd say—since they are probably off celebrating their win.

"You still there?"

She smiles and splashes water on her chest. "Yup."

I nod about a thousand times, drooling over this woman, but I can't seem to stop myself like I did the other night on our call. I'm no longer the strong one. Maybe it's because my defenses are down, and I was caught off guard by Paige in her swimsuit when I called. Regardless, I've completely thrown out my resolve to give her space.

"I'm sorry you lost," she says.

I've already forgotten our game, too focused on what's in front of me. "We'll get our chance," I tell her.

"Ooo, is this competitive Rhodes 2.0?"

"Maybe," I say with a knowing smirk.

"I like it." She grins.

"I like you."

She laughs. "Do you feel better getting that cheesy line out?"

"Much." I laugh, too. I should apologize for saying something, but my lips are loose, heart splayed open. "I've missed talking to you today. Looks like you made it safely. What's Bozeman like?"

"Beautiful." Her tone is wistful as she says this. "It's a valley, so there are quite literally mountains in every direction I look. I can't wait to see how Yellowstone compares tomorrow. And I've basically been listening to the same song on repeat. It just feels right and captures what it's like to be here."

"Which song?"

"'Get Lost in Montana' by Owl City," she replies, then flips her camera to give me a quick view of a strip of mountains in the distance that stretches the expanse of blue in the sky.

When she turns the camera back to her, my favorite view, there are so many words I want to say to her, so many questions and conversations we have yet to explore, but all I can seem to say is, "I miss you."

She smiles at this. "You said that already."

I shake my head. "I said I missed talking to you today."

Her laugh almost does me in, but her words finish me off. "I miss you, too."

"I wish I was there with you." I'm helpless. I can't remember why I don't tell her these things more often. Why am I holding back again?

Nodding, she leans forward, pushing her phone further back. Her chest presses lightly against the wall, accentuating the tops of her breasts. "What would you do if you were?"

I lick my lips. Even the way she asks this is sexy.

There are so many things I could say. I'd stand behind her with my hands circling her waist, kissing her shoulder or the top of her head. I'd play with the ties of her swimsuit and trace the planes of her stomach with my fingers. I'd press her back against the wall and circle her legs around my waist, showing her exactly how much she turns me on.

But I don't get the chance to say any of that because another guy walks into the locker room, smiling at me in acknowledgment. I nod and then look back at my phone, recognition lighting on her face as well.

We can't have this conversation—not here or now—but I need her to know we're coming back to this one. I'm not ready to abandon it.

"I'm going to shower and head home. Can I call you back when I get there? Maybe fifteen minutes?"

She smiles and rests her chin on her folded arms. "Okay."

I comb through my hair. "Will you still be there?"

Please say yes.

"Depends on if your fifteen minutes turns into more," she says. "I'm already starting to sweat in here."

"Give me ten," I say.

She laughs. "Eager much?"

There's a good reason I should hide how I feel, but it escapes me when she's looking at me like this, and I'm feeling some sort of way. So, I look her dead in the eyes and say, "You have no idea."

23

PAIGE

It's been eight minutes since ending my call with Rhodes.

Eight minutes since he looked at me like he hadn't eaten in years. Eight minutes since I decided I *want* him.

My stomach dips again, and a demanding pulse beats between my legs. I haven't felt this much anticipation in a while, and it's killing me. After I said goodbye, the water got too hot just thinking about how he'd answer my simple question.

What would you do if you were?

Who am I? I can't even believe I said that. Those words came out of my mouth, eliciting a response in my body I'm wholly unprepared for here. I'm lying on one of the benches outside, relishing the feel of the sun on my skin and the need in my body, wondering if my feelings are obvious to anyone but me.

Can other people hear how fast my heart is beating?

Do they know how turned on I am?

Are my pheromones evident to anyone else but me?

I hope not.

I close my eyes and then quickly open them to check the time again on my phone.

Two more minutes.

I smile at the thought.

Maybe I should go somewhere more private, like my van, the bathroom, or possibly a secluded corner. But there's no time. It's not like anything is *actually* going to happen. These are just words. Ones that are no longer stuck inside a text exchange like they had been when Rhodes was *Roger Who Cleans*. Instead, they're being said, roaming around like a wild fire in and outside my body.

On second thought, I think this might make *just* words more dangerous since we decided not to entertain anything yet. Am I any different? Have I changed? I feel like I'm starting to. And other than needing to feel his lips on mine again, I find I really want this. I don't need him to fulfill me, but I definitely want him.

"Excuse me," someone says from beside me. "Do you know where the towels are—"

The woman talking to me gasps, and so do I.

I immediately look down at my body in case I'm somehow naked after all these thoughts about Rhodes. I'm not, thankfully, but I know she knows. She has to. Why else would she react like this?

I swallow but don't say a word.

"Is it you?" the woman with tightly coiled curls asks, dripping water beside my pool chair.

"No?" I'm so guilty.

She clutches her chest. "The singer from last night." She starts wiggling her thick hips covered by a barely-there wrap and singing part of a song I'm not familiar with. "You look just like her. It's okay if you're trying to be coy." She leans in and whispers. "I'm good at keeping secrets if you want to be incognito."

I swallow again as she flips her sunglasses down and waggles her brows.

I'm not hiding a secret identity, just harboring really intense feelings for my best friend. So why does it feel like I've committed a crime?

"You sure you're not with the band? Oh, what were their names...Al—no. Trig—not that. Damn it, I can't remember."

I peer up at her, using my hand to block the sun. "I just got into town an hour ago—" My phone starts ringing, and I know it's Rhodes without even looking at the screen. "I'm sorry, I should take—"

"Misfits!" she yells. "It was the Misfits. God, I thought it would never come to me."

I'm waving my phone in front of me. "I'm glad you figured it out, I have to go—"

"Where are you from then?" she asks, all genuine and kind, like she really wants to know.

I'm finding it hard not to match her energy and deny her a simple answer to her question. It'll be quick anyway, so I let Rhodes' call go to voicemail, knowing he'll never leave me one. "Washington State," I say, ready to leave it at that and make my own excuses. But decorum and my people-pleasing tendencies don't allow me to stop there. "And you?"

"Florida." She waves a hand in front of her floral one-piece. "I know it doesn't look like it, me being so pale and all, but I was born and raised there. What brings you to Montana?"

She peers beside me at the empty chair.

Oh no.

My phone starts ringing again just as she asks, "Mind if I sit?"

Yes. "Not at all." She sits, and I ignore Rhodes' call to respond, knowing I might get rid of her faster if I do. "I'm on a...trip."

"A vacation?"

"Not exactly." I tip my head.

"A work trip?"

Still not it. "Like a journey." I really need to figure out a better way to explain this. So, I try again. "Like a self-discovery kind of journey. It doesn't really have an end date."

She clutches her bountiful chest again. "That is so inspiring."

I nod, peering down at the incoming text.

Rhodes:
> I'm back. Call when you can.

A part of me wants to say *screw people pleasing* and get up and walk away. I *really* want to talk to Rhodes. It's like a switch has been flipped, and the friendly dynamic of our relationship is taking on something entirely...feral. I want to see where it will go. But I can't seem to make myself get up now that I'm locked into this social obligation.

And maybe this was the pause I needed to think before acting. Rhodes was dead set on us waiting, even if he seemed to have abandoned all reason on our call today. Maybe I need to be the one to slow things down this time. I don't want to. I don't like it. But I can see the wisdom in it. Plus, starting anything, including some kind of pseudo-physical relationship while I'm hundreds of miles away, doesn't make a lot of sense.

With a new resolve to give some space to my conversation with Rhodes, I ask, "And what brought you here?"

She formally introduces herself as Samantha before she goes into a lengthy description about her sister's husband's brother, who tried to hit on her at the family reunion, and she ended up making out with him. They both booked this trip to be together, only for her to find out he was engaged.

"Oh *no*," I exclaim, fully invested in this daytime *who's the father* Maury TV special. "That sounds awful. I'm so sorry."

She shrugs and leans back against the chair, closing her eyes. "It's okay. He was a great kisser and most men who are have had a few side pieces. If you don't have to teach them even a little, you should run."

I sit stock still and consider this.

Rhodes was a *great* kisser. Like how-are-you-this-good kind. He hasn't had many relationships from what I know, which means...

Shit.

I stare down at his text and reread it.

No.

Rhodes isn't like that. He wouldn't be sleeping with people on the side while saying he liked me all this time.

But that kiss.

I'm immediately transported back to that moment outside Smith's Burgers, where his hands seemed to know the landscape of my body, his tongue sweeping into my mouth, claiming it for its own like he knew how to do it.

I touch my lips again, then look over at Samantha, who still has her eyes closed, chin tipped toward the sun as she talks about the prairie dog town she visited yesterday. I steal the opportunity to respond to Rhodes.

> Me:
> Got held up in a convo at the pool. I'll call you later!

The part of me that questions whether Rhodes has someone on the side is small enough that I'm not sure I should even entertain the idea for long. But then again, I've been on the receiving end of a cheater, and it's terrible. I'd run so fast.

I need a second to think. There are too many competing emotions bouncing around inside my gut and thoughts skating along the synapses of my brain that aren't firing properly.

"We should go out together tonight!" Samantha says exuberantly, flinging her eyes open wide to look at me. "I've been wanting to check out downtown Bozeman."

I really wish I possessed the ability to say the word *no*. "Yeah, we should. It's my birthday tomorrow."

Did I just agree?

"Your birthday?" she screeches. "We have to make this big. Get dressed up, wear heels and lipstick."

I try to kindly back out. "It's only my thirtieth. I was just planning to eat—"

"YOUR THIRTIETH?" Now she's yelling. "That's the biggest birthday you could ever celebrate." Her eyes are wide as she stares at me, placing a solemn hand on her chest again. "It would be the greatest honor to take you out and celebrate your birthday with you."

With this kind of confession, I can't just explain how I was planning to eat Pop-Tarts for dinner and watch a show on my laptop. And maybe it would be kind of fun.

"Okay, yeah. I'd like that," I find myself saying.

"Great!" Samantha dives headfirst into a story about how her friend also kissed the engaged dude she was with and how meeting *good* people is so hard, but she thinks I'm one of them. I can't break her heart by backing out, but maybe I can fake an illness later.

For now, I listen attentively, only letting my thoughts linger on the kiss with Rhodes every few seconds.

The one that has completely changed my entire brain chemistry.

CALLING RHODES BACK before saying goodbye to Samantha became impossible.

Mainly because she gave me a tour of her campground after the hot springs.

The fifth-wheel trailer she's renting locally is ginormous compared to Vincent VanGo. It has four slide-outs and a satellite dish bigger than my windshield. She said someone from the rental company set it up for her before arriving, which also included a full outdoor oasis complete with a full-size barbecue, patio furniture, outdoor rug, and tiki torches.

It's a five-star resort, not a campsite.

We parted ways to change before agreeing to meet outside and get a rideshare to head downtown. She told me not to worry about a thing, and she had everything planned out. Since she literally never had a phone in her hand once, it makes me curious about what she's put together.

There's a part of me that thrills at the idea I won't have to celebrate my birthday alone, even if it is a day early. When I planned this trip, it was the one thing that made me reconsider since I'd be missing out on all of my favorite things.

My family usually takes me to the small Italian restaurant in the town over with red and white tablecloths and low lighting. They'd follow it up with a lemon meringue pie at home, where I'd be forced, regardless of my thirty years on this planet, to make a wish and blow out the candles after they sang a very off-tune rendition of the Birthday song.

Rhodes and Amber would surprise me with an iced coffee and a trip to every thrift store in a thirty-mile radius—and there are a lot—to go shopping. We'd go out to lunch at the all-you-can-eat Mongolian restaurant with mini egg rolls, gyoza, and every sauce imaginable. Some years, we'd all go on an overnight trip, but mostly, it was the simple stuff that made it special.

I won't have any of that this year, which made me want to forgo celebrating.

Until Samantha.

I can't say I'm entirely upset about the plan. It's different, but I think it could also be fun. We really hit it off at the pool while we chatted about ex-boyfriends and our love of thrifting. She seems so wholesome and kind, and what started as an obligatory conversation ended with a familiarity I miss from back home.

If only finding something to wear were as easy as saying *yes*.

I settle on a cropped tank that looks more like a bra with skinny straps and a ribbed texture as well as my Cupid underwear and black denim shorts. My tall brown boots would go well, and I can always bring my longer red blazer to go over it.

Dropping my outfit in front of the kitchen counter, I position my phone on top of the automatic coffee maker to call Rhodes back.

He answers right away. "Paige."

Is it just me, or did he sound out of breath?

"Hi." I squat a little lower, sitting back on my heels and looking more like a floating head while I nervously fidget with my fingers. "I met a new friend, and she wouldn't stop talking to me at the pool. But she actually turned out to be really nice, so we're going to grab some food downtown together—like an early birthday celebration—but I didn't want you to think I didn't want to talk. I did want to talk—*do* want to talk. I was just caught up in this conversation." Up until Rhodes told me how he felt a couple of weeks ago, I would have started changing. It's not like he can see anything, but that doesn't feel right. So, I twist my tank around my wrist.

And second-guess everything.

"Paige," he says again but with a terse tone.

I stop rotating the tank, searching for the elusive tag, and look at him.

He's leaning forward, arms spread wide on his counter like an upside-down V. "Are you wearing a shirt, or bra, something? It's really distracting."

I look down at my swimsuit, my peaked nipples visible through the fabric. "Oh, no. I mean, yes, I am. I was going to change, and then..."

And then remembered I have no idea what I'm doing anymore or if I should give into these whims or not. Keep us firmly in the *friend-only* arena, or offer more. Damn, do I want more.

He nods slowly, methodically, like he's thinking about something but hasn't formed the thought enough to say it.

I consider untying my swimsuit top at my nape, but I don't. I wait. I think. I watch.

"I've seen your bra before, but I haven't—" He stops himself, or maybe the dark gleam in his eyes does. "This is different."

It is. He's right. This territory is so new and foreign in ways I want to know intimately. "Alfredo," I whisper.

Our safe word has always been to trigger the real, unfiltered thoughts we might be thinking but haven't said. In this case, I'm suddenly so curious. I have to know what's going on in his head. I need his words more than anything.

"You...and me. God, Paige, it's all I've been thinking about." He sounds pained. "Seeing you in the water...your swimsuit."

I exhale, my shoulders falling slightly with the action. "I've been thinking about you, too."

"My thoughts haven't exactly been...friendly," he clarifies.

"Not in a friendly way for me, either." I nod. "But this trip—"

"I know," he says, eyes taking an extended blink. "We shouldn't."

"Or..." I offer. "We should."

He studies me, his mouth in a hard line. "What do you mean?"

Before I know what I'm doing, instinct takes over, and I untie the straps around my neck and let them fall. My shoulders and collarbones are the only things visible on the screen, but it's suggestive enough to tell him what I'm thinking.

He stands straighter, bracketing his hips with his hands while he stares me down through the camera. "Your top...Paige."

"It's okay. *I'm* okay. I want this," I say, nearly breathless.

He drops his palms back to the counter, hovering in front of the camera. "Are you sure?"

I don't know if this is a path we should take—if I'm figured out to be enough for him. But I don't see how that wouldn't be possible with how he's looking at me. He doesn't just see me as enough, he sees me as *everything*. Like I could somehow stop the earth from spinning or at least his heart from beating.

"I'm sure."

He licks his lips, studying me for all of my tells he knows to see if I'm lying. But I don't bite my lip or fiddle with my glasses. Assured that I'm not feeding him a line, the grooves between his brows soften, and his expression darkens, voice thick. "Have you used it?"

"Used what?"

He clears his throat. "The vibrator."

My lips part. "How did you—"

"I saw it in one of your bins I carried out. I've been thinking about it every day since."

I've never heard Rhodes talk like this before. Unabashed and so...*blunt*. It's weirdly hot, and I don't want him to stop. I want to know what else he's thinking. I don't want to put my shirt on. I want to take everything else off. I don't want to tip-toe around my feelings while I'm trying to figure out my life.

Maybe I want him in it.

Maybe I want him in me.

"I've used it," I confirm.

He leans forward on his forearms, dropping his voice to a whisper. "Have you thought about me while using it?"

Heat pools between my legs at the thoughts I haven't had but am most certainly conjuring now. "Maybe."

"Paige."

"Rhodes."

"Do you want to? Use it, that is...with me?"

I look down at my half-naked body, the measly bathing suit bottoms covering my lower half that could easily be removed. I could touch myself. He could watch. The van has curtains that are all closed, and the door is already locked. It would be so easy, and by the heat flooding my veins, so right.

But then I think about what Samantha said at the pool.

If you don't have to teach a man how to kiss, he's been kissing too many people.

This isn't just a random FaceTime hook-up. This is *Rhodes*, and I care about these things. I care about who we are and what we become tomorrow.

"I want to," I say quickly, "but Rhodes, why are you such a good kisser? Do you practice...like with other women? You told me you haven't been with a lot of people, but if you have, it's okay if you are. I just want to know."

After hearing Samantha's story, I'm more on edge. I like to think I know Rhodes better than I know myself, but what if I don't? What if...

His brows dive together. "Paige, no. I haven't been seeing anyone. I don't *want* to see anyone else."

"Even casually?" I ask, staring at my lap. "Hooking up—"

"No. I swear to you. I'm not hooking up with anyone."

"Then why are you such a good kisser?" I press, suddenly so desperate to know why this man is so good, so true, so seemingly perfect for me. There has to be a reason.

The corner of his mouth tilts up in a smile, and he stares at me with so much longing, so much desire, I squirm through the camera lens. "Because I was kissing you."

My mouth is suddenly filled with rocks, and I can't manage to say a thing.

Instead, all I want to do is jump him, leap onto his person, and kiss him some more. There isn't a question I'd let him muss me up beyond recognition if he were here.

But we aren't even in the same state.

"And you really think that?" I ask.

"I really do."

I peer at the small bin beneath my bed with odd knick-knacks and random items. "Okay." Searching for the tiny but powerful toy amongst the items, I rummage around and pull the vibrator out, holding it up between two fingers in front of the camera. But I don't use it, not yet.

"*Shit*," he says on an exhale, visibly squirming but never looking away. "How are you going to use that?"

I snap my gaze to the screen. "I think you know."

The next thing I do surprises me. I trail the vibrator across my collarbone and down my neck, further over the plain of my now quivering stomach, pretending it's his hand I'm moving around my body in all the places I crave him most.

"It's you," he says, the words grating on his vocal cords. "Only you."

Flicking it on to a low vibration and lowering it down between my legs, I use my other hand to play with my nipple, tossing my head back as though he's the one touching me. I know what his hands look like, his fingers, too, what they would feel like flitting over my slick center.

I'm already so turned on, a mess of need for him, with only the familiar resonance of his voice filling my van and my veins. "Tell me what you're doing," he says gruffly. "It's on vibrate. I'm touching my—"

There's a knock on my door, and I startle. I meet his wide eyes through the screen, and it seems all we can do is stare blankly, waiting for the person on the other side of the door to ruin everything.

"Don't. Go," he says quietly, then adds, "Please."

His steely eyes keep me rooted to the spot, but I flip the vibrator off, and it's the loudest noise in the whole van. I don't know how he liked me for so long and said or did nothing about it. We probably could have been doing this a lot sooner. But now, an interruption has stopped us once again.

"It's Samantha!" the voice calls.

"Just a moment," I say.

Rhodes shakes his head and bites his fist.

The heat between my legs has already turned to pounding. Rhodes did this, and I don't want to leave this van without finishing.

"I'll be over in ten minutes!" I call back.

"I can just wait here," she says.

I shake my head, biting the sides of my tongue. "That's okay! You don't have to."

"I don't mind."

Rhodes shakes his head, and I give him an apologetic look.

"Please, Paige," he mouths, trying to stay quiet.

"Tonight. Later," I tell him, then end the call before I decide to give him a show with Samantha's voice as background music.

I'm still topless, halfway to getting dressed before I was interrupted. I have an idea that is so High School Paige, I barely recognize it.

I could send him a picture.

I've done it before, and Rhodes won't share it with anyone.

It would probably make up for the cock block from seconds before.

It's brilliant, really.

I position the phone just so, turning the camera on and pointing it at me. I try a few positions until I feel like one sticks. One hand cups the opposite boob with my forearm just blocking the other nipple. I set the timer for three seconds, then hook a thumb in my bottoms and tug them down a little.

It isn't magazine-worthy, but it's the raciest Rhodes has ever seen me.

I check the picture and debate taking a couple more to test the lighting and angle again, but I decide not to edit myself and send it off as is. Even I'm a little hot thinking about what he'll do with this picture. Maybe I should make it a requirement that he tell me.

Sending it off, I also add:

Me:
I want to know exactly what you do with this.

24

Rhodes

A text comes through the second I set my phone down on the kitchen counter, and I wonder if it's Paige changing her mind. A man can hope.

Instead, it's a photo that immediately has me dropping my phone on the floor as if it's on fire, and I suppose it sort of is.

Paige.

Is.

Naked.

Mostly.

"Fuck," I say out loud, covering my mouth with one hand as I try to absorb what is on my phone screen.

Paige:
> I want to know exactly what you do with this.

A weird noise I don't recognize leaves my mouth as my entire sense of decorum and friendliness leaves my body in a rush. What I *want* to do is nothing close to what I probably should. I'm turned on and thinking only with the reptilian part of my brain that says I need her *right the fuck now*.

But I can't do that.

I can't have her the way I want.

This picture is a damn close second, however. The way her hand is lazily covering her nipple, exposing most of her beautiful breast, is delicious. She's bare and vulnerable, and I've never been more turned on. No cold shower or pickleball tournament will rid me of this feeling, the one sparking in my heart and lower.

I'm aimlessly shuffling around my apartment with no real destination, only the need to keep moving. Sensation climbs my spine and catapults off as I stare, licking and biting my lower lip as I think.

I want to lick her from her head to her toes, devouring every part of her.

I want to print this picture and frame it on my wall if it were appropriate.

I want to listen to the blood flow pooling in my dick.

I want so much more than this, but mostly, I want her on the phone with me when I tell her all of these things. I don't want to just think them.

I'm done doing that.

We've stepped out of best friend land and have entered a far more exciting place with possibility. But she's going out tonight and completely unavailable for hours. If she wasn't, I'm sure we'd be well on our way to third base via video chat.

There's one part of my rational brain that screams out with questions.

Why is she sending you this?

Does this mean she wants a relationship?

Is she ready?

Am I?

I keep staring at the photo, tapping my screen when it tries to go dark as I stop pacing. I'm going to waste all of my battery just by looking at this photo all night. But should I? Can I? When I had her on the phone, it didn't bother me. I was ready to dive headfirst into phone sex—something I've never done before—without any real context. But now, I have a chance to consider everything.

Damn brain.

Paige said she wanted to find herself on this trip. It's why she left. It's why she left *me*. And while a very large part of me wants to continue talking and pursuing her as if my rationale is controlled by a throbbing extremity, I don't want her to have any regrets.

Wondering *why* might be the most torturous part of being human.

So, as much as I want to strip down below the waist and relieve this building ache screaming at me, to tell Paige exactly how many times I'm going to jack off to this photo, I need to know *why*. I need to let the love I have for her speak louder than my desire.

Saving the photo, I quickly text her back. And by quickly, it's likely been five minutes of writing and deleting everything I've tried to say. I finally end up with:

Me:
> We need to talk about this.

She doesn't respond right away. I imagine she and her new friend are together, preparing to go out tonight where anything could happen. Part of me believes she could wake up the next morning and hate me. Rational Rhodes laughs with a baritone sound like a haughty British man. It's not true, but putting myself out there with Paige after all this time has had me on the outskirts of my control for weeks.

According to Amber, I've tipped, and I'm already drowning.

My heart jumps into my throat when my phone vibrates, and she responds.

Paige:
> Did you not like it?

And cue the *shit*.

Me:
> That's not what I meant.

Me:
> I love it.

I love you.

But I can't unload that here. Not like this.

Me:
> But I need to know what this means.

Paige:
> It means, "Have a good night."

There's no way I won't, but it still doesn't answer my question.

Me:
> I meant what does this mean for us?

She's not as quick to respond, but when she does, I'm not sure if it should give me hope or not.

Paige:
> Can I call you tomorrow morning?

Me:
> Yeah, of course. Happy birthday, Paige.

She doesn't respond regardless of how many minutes I let tick by waiting.

I scroll back to my photos and scratch at my jaw, warring with myself over what I should do and what I want to do. Instead of getting off the couch to get my laptop and do some more video editing, maybe order myself dinner, I'm toying with the idea of staying right here with this picture. She's so sexy, I don't even think she realizes. So many douchebags have lined up to be with her, likely only seeing her as this photo portrays.

But I see more.

There's a small scar just above one of her ribs where she had a freak accident when she was twelve while rollerblading and fell on a stick. It cut through her flimsy tank and made her bleed. I was the one who procured a band-aid for her, delicately dabbing the wound with a wet paper towel and fanning it until it dried enough to put the bandage on.

Her fingernails are painted every color of the rainbow, a decision she likely made purely because she couldn't decide which color to go with. So she chose them all. She's also wearing the braided gold ring her parents got her for high school graduation on her middle finger, the same place it's always lived.

All of these things make up Paige, the woman I love. The one who is as sexy on the inside as the outside, which is why I'm going to try really hard to wait until tomorrow to do anything about this picture.

I don't want to start with any regrets.

I don't want to be like the others.

Maybe we should wait until we're in person again before exploring so much of our physical relationship. This time of her being away means something; I don't want to rush that process for her or me.

Turning off my screen, I stand and pocket my phone, guarding her vulnerability. I have to adjust myself, the uncomfortable bulge in my jeans making it near impossible to stay committed to the cause of talking to Paige before I degrade that picture with every last bit of lust I have in my body.

I think I need a therapist.

But for tonight, I make myself a cup of tea, letting the peppermint sting my senses while I open to a blank page in my journal and write *Dear Paige* at the top.

25

Paige

Samantha is one hell of a woman.

She's been verbally writing me her memoir, which undoubtedly would make all of the bestsellers lists as well as rights to its own TV series. We're at the part of the story where her father sold their childhood dog to the circus so he could buy a drum set.

She was eight.

We still have twenty years to go, and I'm already three drinks, an eggplant tahini spread with flatbread, and a campfire doughnut in.

I'll be ancient by the time we finish. Cleo will think I'm dead and not returning. The two bowls of cat food, one small plate of wet food, and three water bowls I left for her will only last tonight.

After catching a ride downtown and walking around for a bit, we settled on this place, an underground restaurant with Noir vibes. Dark lighting sets the mood while jewel tones of rubies, greens, and golds splash across wallpaper, furniture, and accent decor. All of it was so unsuspecting since it's below street level.

I finish off my dessert and push the plate away, debating on whether to order more food while I listen. Samantha has other plans, though, since she turns the conversation to me.

"Do you have a boyfriend?" she asks, sipping her fruity cocktail with extra maraschino cherries bobbing around in it.

I freeze up, not expecting this question to be turned on me so soon, if at all. We've already talked at length about her ex, who I also discovered procures feet pics on the side and sells them. I naturally had a lot of questions about this.

She's staring at me with her full attention now; chin propped on her clasped hands with elbows digging into the glass table top.

It's suddenly so hot down here. "I don't have an official boyfriend."

Look at me being a grown-up.

"Are you sleeping with him?" she asks bluntly.

I tilt my head, thinking of the half-nude photo I sent of myself earlier. Rhodes said he really liked it, but his text message made it seem like something was on fire. Like maybe I shouldn't have done it. Let's just hope it was his pants that were burning and not his mind. Rhodes, with a nagging thought, is no good.

"Not exactly."

Samantha's brows pinch together. "I don't think I'm tracking."

"He's my *not yet*."

This doesn't seem to ease the wrinkles between her brows.

I'm not one to undershare, so I immediately launch into another full explanation, ending with: "There's no way I can tell Amber about the photo because *nude*, and I'm starting to think I crossed a line by doing that. I came on this trip to figure myself out, spend time on my own being independent, and finding out what I want to do about a career. But now I'm starting to think that was a tall order. How am I supposed to fit that all into weeks when it could take a lifetime?" I take a breath. "I really like him, and I don't want to wait too long or too little."

"You're overthinking this," Samantha says. "Sounds to me like you just need to get laid."

My mouth gapes, and I peer around the small room to see if anyone might have heard this. "I can't sleep with a random person I don't know. That's...reckless."

"I didn't say random," she clarifies. "I'm sure Mr. Not Yet would love to finish what you started with that picture you sent him."

That's the problem.

I want that.

I want it so badly, I'm afraid of just how much. Seeing his sweet face morph into something darker, something more unruly, like a feral cat in heat. Opening the door a crack has me so curious what the room inside looks like.

"There's just so much pressure to do this right for our sakes. I don't want him to be just another guy I date and dump. I want it to last, but I need to dial in what else I really want. Rhodes has his life figured out. A good career, a level head, and a tool set he knows how to use."

She holds a hand out. "Okay, wow. Breathe."

I take another deep breath, doing as she says. "It's a lot, I know."

"It is, but it isn't as complicated as you're making it out to be." Her dark curls bounce as she says this.

This wouldn't be the first time I'd done this.

"Do you think I have all my shit figured out? I'm in the middle of a love triangle—"

"Wait, you are?" I don't remember her telling me this.

She hooks a thumb over her shoulder. "Yeah, a couple of guys at the hot springs had it out for me, but I told them both it was a strong maybe."

I'm sure my mouth is open.

"Anyway, I think there's this myth that truly decent humans who are trying to change themselves don't deserve good things. Life isn't an obstacle course with a direct path to the finish line." She picks up her drink with a flashing ice cube and two straws. "It's more like a maze. Sometimes you start out on the right path and end up getting it wrong. But you don't just quit. You try a different direction."

Holy shit, this is making so much sense.

How does she know how to do this? Asking questions like this causes me to think. My head is spinning at how much sense it all makes and how much pressure I've put on myself...how much The Itch has affected my life. When in reality, I just needed to take a step. Traveling across states was a big one, but that's kind of my style.

"This man clearly loves you from all that you said. He's your good thing. So, do you love him?"

I swallow, but the truth lodges in my throat. "I...don't know."

Her expression softens, not out of pity but understanding. "Have you let yourself love him? Because it sounds like you're hung up on a journey that doesn't end until you—" She draws a line across her throat with her finger.

I study the table, every nick and crevice of the wood beneath the smooth glass top with my fingerprints blurring it. "I don't think I have."

She leans closer over the table. "It sounds like this is an age-old case of seeing yourself as unworthy of his love, so you don't even let yourself consider it."

My mouth falls open yet again, and I stare directly at her, but she appears to be swaying. Granted, my head is already a little swirly from the drinks. "Holy shit, Samantha. You're like a therapist."

She smiles broadly. "I've seen enough of them."

We both laugh until we've garnered the attention of the waitress again, and she refills our drinks once more, saying they're *on the house* since she finds out it's my birthday tomorrow. I can't stop laughing when Samantha borrows my glasses, propping them on the tip of her nose while she pretends to write notes in my pretend chart. And I keep laughing while drunkenly stumbling back up the stairs to street level again because apparently four cocktails at twenty-nine mean the same at thirty: drunk off my ass.

But on the ride back to the campground where Samantha continued her charade as a shrink for our driver, and maybe Rhodes since I think we called him, I had a thought. A thought that plagued me when I was fumbling into my van—which I realized the next morning was actually Samantha's trailer—that maybe I just need to let myself love Rhodes. Maybe I need to stop thinking I have to be someone or do something to feel deserving of his love. True love. Not a fling or a good time. But for always.

The thought is big and weighty as it dances across my thoughts, but it's hard to grab hold of. I blame it on cocktail number three.

With my cheek plastered to the high-end linoleum floor in Samantha's rig and the under-cabinet lighting that burns my retinas when my eyes are open, I think of only one thing. It's another journal entry I hope I remember enough to write tomorrow.

I see myself writing it as I drift. It starts the same way it always does, but it ends with a confession I'm not sure I'm ready to hear or know quite what to do with. But that's the point of journals. You can write whatever you want, admit the truths that feel the most raw and undefined. The kinds of things that warrant being kept under lock and key.

Except this one, I'll let him read one day.

Dear Rhodes, I think I love you.

26

CLEOCATRA

I think my human has forgotten about me.
   No matter.
I'll claw my way out of here if I need to.
I'm a predator, a fact she keeps forgetting.
The feather toy I've killed could tell her as much...
If it were alive.

27

RHODES

It's Sunday, and in order to avoid waiting around for Paige's call, I woke up early to get to the gym. I played pickleball with the wall for a while, lifted some weights until that wasn't enough, and decided to run a casual five miles on the treadmill.

I can't remember the last time I ran that much, but it was warranted.

I thought getting my mind off the photo and having a conversation with Paige about it was the only thing I'd wake up worried about today. Or the fact I'm a chump who can't seem to handle himself when a woman sends a nude.

Well, I can't.

Because this is *Paige*.

But regardless of how difficult it is to get out of the shower after working out, careful not to touch or linger any place while soaping up, all I'm thinking about is *her*.

Not the *her* from the photo, but the *her* that I hope made it home okay last night after her drunken call. I could barely make out her words through the heavy slur, and her friend Samantha kept asking how I feel about things like a shrink. I'm guessing it was some kind of inside joke between them since it sent Paige into a fit of giggles every time, especially when Samantha asked if I'd be paying by check or card.

There wasn't a reason for the call that I could tell. And even though I told Paige to text me when she got back to her van safely, I never heard from her. So, my mind went to the worst-case scenarios, obviously.

Trampled by wild animals.

Stolen by a cowboy.

Thrown into prison.

Or—my personal hell—in a hospital somewhere.

I tell myself what my new therapist encouraged when I started feeling worded up: *breathe*. I've only had one session, but so far, it's helping me process the things I can't control. It's the first time I've ever seen someone, but luckily, he's had plenty of patients like me.

So, I breathe in. And when I count to seven and exhale, I breathe in again.

The dressing room has quite a few people in it despite it being Sunday, but I barely notice them while I change and towel dry my hair. Slinging my gym bag over my shoulder, I toss my towel in the bin by the exit and trudge to the swinging front doors to get to the elevator. My finger isn't even off the button for floor five when Paige's name lights up my phone screen.

I inhale through my nose to relax first, then I quickly answer. "Paige."

"Sorry it took so long to call," she starts. "I woke up on Samantha's floor, and it took three eggs, bacon, and an ungodly amount of coffee to come alive again. I'm on the road now, so if you hear me curse, it's because the sun is being annoyingly bright."

I lean against the back wall of the elevator, bracing a hand on the bar, relieved she's safe and wasn't recruited by a rodeo circuit. "You had a good birthday celebration then?"

"I did. Samantha really made it a good one. You know, despite the hangover."

"It sounded like you had a good time." The elevator steadily climbs as silence fills the line. "Do you remember anything about last night?"

"Nope," she says, but doesn't continue.

"Nothing?" I'm glad her night was prison-free.

The doors split, opening up to my floor. The thin carpet squares mute any sound my footfalls make, but I'm not sure I can say the same about my heart currently thundering in my chest. I know the conversation about the photo is coming.

"I mean...I remember dinner, the drinks, the story of Samantha's first kiss. There were three guys involved, which I'm finding is a thing for her, but it's too early to revisit that one." The music she has playing softly in the background cuts off. "Just out of curiosity, did I...say anything to you? Like information that would be best said when I'm not drunk?"

I slip my key into the lock and turn. "Like when you asked me to lie down and tell you all of my fears?"

"Not that...more like personal things."

I wrack my brain to try and remember every piece of our conversation, which I've been doing all morning, but I can't think of anything she might have said that she clearly wishes she hadn't.

"Can't remember anything personal unless you consider inviting your Uber driver to your birthday party as personal." I'm trying really hard not to laugh. "But I've got time now if you wanted to tell me."

"No!" she shouts. "Nope...no, I'm good. I should...you know. Let me get back to you on that."

A small laugh escapes me. "Alright. Top secret, got it."

There's so much more I want to ask, but she'll tell me if she really wants to. My thoughts keep moving to the enormous conversation we should have. Another long pause persists as I drop my keys and bag and move directly for the fridge to make a smoothie.

"About last night," she says. "The first part where I wasn't delusional."

My entire body ignites, and I immediately expect the worst. "Yeah?"

Did my voice just squeak?

"I'm sorry for sending you that photo without...context."

Context, yes. "Mhm."

She sighs and continues. "After talking to Samantha about it, I realized some things. First, I don't think I've allowed myself to be known by someone—vulnerable and all that. I've been waiting for things to change for me when I could probably go after it more. You're just so put together. Like a complete adult who knows how to do taxes and clean out their car. I want to be better for you," she says somberly, "and me."

I can barely breathe. "You really think this about me? Paige, I'm the one who doesn't feel worthy. You are...everything. All of the good and beautiful things in this life. You have a perspective I dream of. A way of holding things loosely and rolling with any change that comes. I'm nowhere close to being as flexible as you are. I could stand for living a little more and controlling every aspect of my life a lot less."

She stutters when she speaks. "I-I didn't know you thought all of this about me."

A problem I want to remedy. "I spent too much time *not* telling you a lot of things. A fact I regret."

"It's not like I made it easy on you. I ran away, and I realize now that a part of me needed to do this to come to the conclusions I have, but I don't want to keep running away. I know I've got room to grow, things to figure out. But what I'm trying to say is that I'm not very good at fully opening myself up. I don't even know what that looks like, but I want to try. I guess that's why I sent you that picture. I want to reach out, but

I don't know how. I think I was vulnerable in the wrong ways. So, I'm sorry."

"First off, there's no need to apologize for the photo."

"Really?" she presses.

"I mean, we pushed things further than we ever have before, but that doesn't warrant an apology. I don't ever want you to feel you have to apologize for being vulnerable in any capacity." I pace my kitchen, smoothie forgotten. "I just didn't know if it was for the hell of it or because you were ready to be with *me*. Once I had a chance to think, I realized I didn't want this just to be physical. I'll wait for however long you need me to until you figure things out, but please know that there isn't a single thing you could do that would change my mind about you. I love who you are today." Warmth floods my body. "I love the Paige who wears nothing and makes every part of me painfully turned on."

"Painfully, huh?"

"You have no fucking idea."

She laughs. "Maybe a little."

"I love the Paige who also chooses to sew a full outfit on a whim. I fell for the woman who rewatches *Parks and Rec* episodes, laughing at the same scenes like it's the first time she's seen them. You're the woman I want to tell everything to and know everything about. There isn't a second I stop thinking about you, which I'm starting to wonder if I should at least have a minute to think about other things."

She giggles from her end of the line, but I feel it in every pore.

"I want all of you," I admit, feeling more free than I have in weeks. "The known and unknown. The messy and undecided parts that make you human. You don't have to figure out your life on your own, Paige. I'm not scared off by the question marks."

The soft sniffles on her end of the line make it sound like she's crying or at least holding back tears. "I want you, too. I want us to try this together, but I may not be good at loving you or have life fully figured out like you. I want you to teach me."

My fist punches through the air, the smile on my face so wide, I can't hide the elation in my voice. "I can do that. As long as you promise to teach me how to loosen up a little."

"Deal." She laughs. "Are you fist-punching the air?"

"Maybe." A smile lights my entire face, my entire self.

I have a chance—a shot with Paige. It's what I've always wanted. And now I'm holding it. The bid for connection and openness isn't lost. I hold it reverently with both hands.

We talk until her service gets spotty and the drive becomes so windy that she has to focus on the road. So, for safety's sake, we reluctantly hang up, and for the first time since I discovered I had feelings for this woman, my heart seems at peace, no longer wandering through a remote desert without water. I'm immersed in these new emotions and even newer revelations.

Paige is my person, and despite there being more we have to sort in ourselves, I'm convinced—delusional even—that we can.

I just wish it could've stayed this way.

28

Paige

I understand now why people visit Yellowstone.

The landscape rolls on for miles at a time in all directions, and the sun always seems to know which angle is the best to highlight the beauty of it all. Whoever said Wyoming was flat never visited because it's full of rocky clefts and deep valleys. Sure, they aren't mountain peaks covered in evergreens, but they are stunning in their own right, full of different colored rock faces.

Not many people realize—me included—that Montana only claims a sliver of the top portion of the park compared to Wyoming. Sure, Bozeman, Montana, is the best place to fly into, but Wyoming holds the majority of this precious land.

I started in West Yellowstone this morning, holding up the line of cars with no two license plates being the same when I had to hop out and take a selfie with the Yellowstone National Park sign. I wasn't the only one. Tons of people were snapping photos, even if the background scenery only included a paved road and skinny alders.

Rhodes has never been to Yellowstone, either, so I made sure to send him every photo I took so he could experience it with me—even the blurry ones.

He doesn't seem to mind.

He's liked every single one, adding in emojis and voice notes, too.

After pulling off to one of the rest stops inside the park, I hop back in my van and leash up Cleo so she can explore, too. She immediately finds a rock thrice her size to jump on, perched like a killer, ready to pounce on anything that moves.

There's a waterfall behind the restrooms with a path leading closer. I tug Cleo so I can read the sign and see what I'm looking at, but she refuses to move, chattering to the wildlife that she is armed with claws and ready to destroy something. So I people-watch instead.

The park is incredibly diverse. The stark contrasts of all the different colors and languages are expected now. Full conversations are happening all around without me knowing what they mean. Maybe it's the land's beauty, or someone has gum on the bottom of their shoe they can't get off. *Oh.* And the clothes everyone wears range from designer and brand name to rain poncho—it's not raining—making for an eclectic mix of people.

I wore my Chacos, jean shorts, and a Yellowstone T-shirt I picked up as a birthday gift to myself at one of the ranger stations. I slipped it on at the last bathroom stop. I'm positive I've seen the same one on at least ten different people. But I still smile and throw a thumbs-up of approval when I notice.

Earlier, I spoke to a woman in the checkout line who is from Canada and has visited different parts of Yellowstone every summer for the last ten years. It's still one of the *most magnificent places she's ever experienced*, she touted. Glacier was their favorite stop with icy blue water from the clean mountain run-off.

I'll have to make a point to go there next year. A promise I make to myself to keep exploring even if I'm settled in life and not traveling in a van.

One thing I wasn't expecting was how spread out everything is. I likely won't be able to see everything within the couple of days I have here—a feat that was hard to come by since most campgrounds were already booked—so I'll have to be particular. Camping near Yellowstone Lake will give me a chance to cover more ground, though.

While Cleocatra makes her chirping noise she only does when hunting, I try to snap a photo and send it to Rhodes, but it won't go through. The service is spotty, sometimes taking up to fifteen minutes to send one photo. I guess I'll just have to accept his delayed reaction and enjoy the view in real-time.

Cleo hasn't moved from her rock, downright refusing, so I scoop her up and decide it's time to keep going. I overhear someone in line for the bathroom mention a herd of bison just up the way, and I'm eager to see them.

We both get back in the van, buckling in for safety, and pull out of the parking lot. Of course, this is the busy season since the weather is perfect, and the snow from winter is long gone except for perpetually shaded areas on certain peaks, so this takes a while. Once I'm on the two-lane road, the traffic seems to stop completely.

Great.

Cleo is already fast asleep in the backseat, clearly uninterested in the fact I rolled down the passenger window for her. But I hang my arm out mine, tapping a rhythm into the side as I wait to inch forward.

And...nothing.

No movement.

We haven't moved an inch in twenty minutes. I also haven't seen any cars pass by us going in the opposite direction. Something's got to be up.

Before I can investigate, a white and green ranger truck slowly creeps down the other lane with flashing yellow lights and words of encouragement for all of us:

"Do not get out of your vehicles. Bison crossing in progress. I repeat, do not get out of your vehicles."

Just as he says this, I can see a few large brown heads with protruding horns and long beards at their chins swaying as they walk slowly. The tops of their noggins can be seen over a couple of the cars, and they seem to be taking up both the center of the road and shoulder, boxing our lane of cars in with their imposing bodies.

Naturally, someone decides to get out of their car, doing the exact opposite of what the ranger said to do, and no, it wasn't me. I made sure to follow the Tourons of Yellowstone social media page prior to coming on this trip after a rabbit-hole search led me to a whole host of potential mishaps. The page is dedicated to actual video footage of people doing the unthinkable: touching the hydrothermal water, attempting to pet or get within twenty-five feet of any animal, climbing rocks they have no business scaling, and the most common, straying off the marked path.

I laughed a lot while binge-watching all of their content, thinking no one *really* does this kind of stuff.

Well, they do, and I'm witnessing it now.

The man and another woman follow suit, stepping out of their cars to get a better look and an even better picture. Do they know how far a bison can launch a human body? It's far, according to the internet, and it does not look pleasant in the slightest. I'm talking you're-getting-airlifted-out-of-here unpleasant.

Peering at my phone, I see two bars of service, so I call Rhodes.

He answers on the first ring. "Are you calling to read me another informational sign at a rest stop?"

I scoff. "No, but it sounds like you didn't enjoy the five-minute reading about the history of that one ravine."

"It was...enlightening."

"Noted," I say. "No, I called because I'm stuck in my van during a bison crossing, and a couple of people decided to get out of their cars."

It's timely since the ranger starts yelling over the loudspeaker: "Get back in your vehicles!"

They do not listen.

He yells again and louder.

"He's really letting them have it," Rhodes says, sucking in a breath through his teeth.

"This is better than watching the videos online. I get a front-row seat to how this actually plays out in real life."

Except, it's far less exciting.

They all get back in their vehicles after the public shame becomes too much. Or because the ranger somehow pushes his truck through the center of the cars like Moses parting the Red Sea. Just in time, too, since the bison herd is navigating through vehicles like the giant, wild beasts they are.

They are getting closer, and *wow*, they are huge.

And cute.

"The show's over. They got back in their cars, but these bison...I think I want one. How about a bison for a souvenir?"

"How about you just get a magnet shaped like a bison?" he suggests.

I laugh. "I would never touch one, considering they live outside and all, but they look fuzzy and soft, like you could curl up next to them and get lost in all the fluffy hair."

AND THE BABIES.

There are two of them that I can see as they move closer, albeit slowly, and they are precious. Caramel-colored fur, sans horns, with little heads and lithe bodies.

"There are babies, Rhodes!" I can definitely see why someone would want to pet a baby.

But that would mean immediate death.

The large mama gets closer, and I push the automatic window button on my van in case she sees me looking at her little babe and decides she doesn't like it.

The window doesn't budge.

"Rhodes," I say, slight fear creeping into my words. "My window won't work."

"What do you mean?"

"The button..."

I keep pressing, over and over, until I'm convinced it's broken. All I hear is the click of the button as I press it incessantly, harder each time. But the lead bison is now at the hood of my van, stopping only long enough to smell something.

It's my panic.

That's what she smells.

I keep trying to put my window up, but it isn't working. "Stay down, Cleo!"

"Shit, Paige, are you okay? What's going on?"

Peering into the back, I realize I attached Cleo's harness to the seat. She's not going anywhere, and it's one less thing to worry about.

"Oh, God, Oh God." The bison's head easily reaches above my side mirror, and this thing is massive. The head alone likely weighs more than this vehicle. "Rhodes!"

"Paige!"

"Stay calm," the ranger yells through the intercom. Unfortunately, the yelling only makes me more nervous.

The bison raises her wet, black nose to my window, and I *scream*. The kind of scream that says I'm trapped and about to die.

"Paige!" Rhodes yells over and over in my ear. "Where are you? What's going on? Can you get help? Talk to me!"

"Bison!" is all I have the ability to say as she licks my door with her creepily long black tongue, her sharp horn knocking against my mirror.

The park ranger is off to the side of the road now, like a few other people, trying to get out of the beast's way, but unfortunately, he's stuck, too, and can't help right now.

I yelp again; this time, it's high-pitched and shrieking.

"Are you hurt?" Rhodes yells. "What can I do? Answer me, please!"

But I can't answer him, too stunned and shocked this is even happening. Why me? Why my van?

The large animal starts to push its body against my van door, shaking my vehicle while it uses it as a scratching post.

"Rhodes! Help! You have to help me!"

"Paige, I need you to focus. Where are you right now?"

I scream even more when the rocking intensifies. Grabbing for the door handle for something to hold onto, I forget my phone is in my hand. It slips out and hits the lip of my window sill, making a slow dive to the pavement below.

I may not be crazy enough to touch a bison, but I blame the shock when I look out my window just in time to see the back hoof of the bison step directly on my phone as it passes by. Unfazed. Uncaring. Totally oblivious. Apparently it was done terrorizing my vehicle, but now my phone has been smashed to smithereens.

Oh no.

Rhodes!

29

RHODES

"Paige!" I scream again even though the line has been disconnected.

My entire body lights up with awareness and buckets of adrenaline. The kind that has you lifting full-size cars off someone in an accident. Everything collides: the questions, the lack of answers, the fear roiling in my gut uncomfortably.

I dial Amber for no other reason than to confirm what I already know. When she answers, she can barely get a word in. "Hello—"

"Paige is in danger," I state, rushing to my closet to get a bag. "She called while waiting in a bison crossing—"

"You know how weird that sounds, right?"

"Just listen!" I grind out through a clenched jaw. "The bison got closer, and she started screaming, and asking me to help her, but the line went dead. Something's wrong, and I'm going to find her. I need you to call the ranger station and see if they found anyone with her description. Check the news. Call the hospital."

"Holy shit. Rhodes, what are you going to do—"

"I'm going to find her." I cut her off and hang up.

I don't even know what I've thrown into my bag; I just know it's packed, and I have to struggle to close the zipper. It's only eleven in the morning, and I have no idea if I can get a flight this last minute to

Bozeman, but I pull up my app while snatching my keys and walking out the door.

I can't even remember if I locked it.

30

PAIGE

My head hurts.

I've been nursing a headache for the last hour after the park ranger started making weird noises through his intercom. I didn't even hear them until after my phone was destroyed.

Of course, there wasn't just *one* bison that passed through the vehicles.

It was close to *one hundred*.

And about half of them stepped on or kicked my phone around as they went.

I couldn't get out of my van, so I sat by and watched through the safety of my closed window, which finally began to work.

Poor Rhodes is probably freaking out, calling every person we both know to see if I reached out to them, too. I haven't. He was the only one. I really need to get to a phone and call him, but I doubt my mostly primitive campground will have one I can use.

After the mass crossing, the cars started moving again, but I pulled to the side of the road to gather some wits and figure out a plan. I didn't even bother trying to recover my destroyed cell. All of my pictures, my evidence that I took this trip on my own, are *gone*. I try not to cry while studying the printed map a ranger handed me at the entrance to find a spot that will have a phone.

Cry later.

The plan was originally to head south toward Old Faithful and loop around to my campground near Yellowstone Lake. I'd continue driving north up the Yellowstone River the next day, ending in Mammoth and exiting out of the north entrance.

I was halfway to the Old Faithful village when I was rudely accosted by the herd of bison, so if I just get there, I know they have a hotel and small shops where I can probably find a phone.

Setting the map down beside me, I get a whiff of something awful.

"What died?" I muse, looking around my cab only to come back to me. I gingerly lift my arm to get a good sniff, and I don't even have to lift it all the way up to know. "It's definitely me."

I might need to beg a shower off the hotel or get a room there in order to use one. It wouldn't be the worst idea I've had. Staying in a luxury hotel after days on the road sounds glorious. It is my birthday, after all.

Just get to the hotel.

I reach for my keys in the ignition.

However, the engine doesn't turn over or roar to life.

More like sputters.

Then dies completely.

And *shit*.

I check my fuel gauge to see how absolutely fucked I am. *Yup*. I'm *out of gas* screwed. The bison crossing took longer than expected, and I never turned the van off, thinking it would clear sooner than it did. Plus, the AC felt too good.

And here I sit, stuck on the side of the road with no gas and no way to reach anyone for help. Rhodes is now Poor Rhodes in my head because I feel horrible for alerting him with my many screams of distress. I wasn't dying, but he didn't know that.

Damn. This is so bad.

The man I love probably thinks I'm dead.

Love.

It's the one thing I've been keeping from him, waiting for the right time to mention it. But it just hasn't felt right to tell him over the phone, regardless of how deeply I feel it. The changes and how my heart wants to jump in his lap and purr like a cat.

Now, I wish I would have said something if only because I'm dramatic, and it feels like I'll never get the chance, at least not for the next few hours.

I stare directly through my front windshield, grabbing the steering wheel with both hands to steady myself. "I love Rhodes."

Saying it out loud doesn't have the kind of effect I want it to. It doesn't relieve the pressure building behind my breastbone or ease the anxiety pulsing in my fingertips to tap his contact and call him.

I need to tell him.

I swallow, but my throat is tight, and my head is light and airy. If I die before getting to tell him this, it will be the most tragic story of all time. I can't let that happen. I need evidence. I need to chisel our initials into a tree or leave a message in a bottle.

That's it.

Something better, far less labor intensive as carving our initials.

I close my gaping mouth and drop my hands from the wheel. "I need my journal."

Cleo doesn't appear to care that we're stuck, continuing to snooze in her bucket seat while I trip all the way back to my bed, where I left my journal. My hands fumble for it, dropping it on the bed before I clumsily whip out the pen and turn to a blank page, starting to write while standing.

Dear Rhodes, I start and don't stop until I've filled an entire page.

I begin to write him some sort of goodbye letter, something I'm not really good at, mixed with a full confession of my love. It was an abrupt turn, but desperate times and all that.

I write everything my heart tells me to, crossing off extra words and adding in letters I forgot to write in my haste to get the words out, which makes the page look cluttered and chaotic, just like my feelings. I'm writing frantically for what seems like hours since when I look through the windshield again, the sun looks dimmer, and my hand is sore.

Spent of all my words, I'm no closer to getting actual help, but I feel lighter. My stomach growls loudly, and the eyes look at me judgmentally, saying, *you should have taken better care of yourself.*

Fine. I'll eat first, then get help.

Grabbing a pack of wipes on the counter, I tug one out to swipe under my armpits before squatting down to open my cooler. The new smell I swear isn't me anymore, is horrendous, and I'm all too aware that I forgot to get ice this morning before leaving the hot springs. I was so jacked up to call Rhodes and start driving that I completely spaced. But now it smells like something died and then rotted and died again, and all the items are grossly warm.

Minus a couple of tangerines I put on the top that are protected by their skin. I grab both, then rummage through the small cabinet beside the water tank to look for what I have left.

I find...crackers.

Really? That's it? I'm supposed to survive on love, two oranges, and some crackers? The only other things in here are Cleo's treats, wet food, and a bag of dry cat food I wouldn't eat in my most daring moments.

The light in the van starts to fade, the sun hiding behind the billowy clouds of Wyoming, and I wonder if I should stand outside and wave down a car in order to use their phone to get help. But now that the traffic has cleared, passersby are intermittent at best. So, instead, I peel open one orange and eat three slices, savoring them as if they'll be my last meal. They might be, at least for a while. Then, without changing into pajamas, I crawl into bed and tell myself I need to think.

Three minutes later, my eyes start to droop.

I love Rhodes is the last thought I have before falling fast asleep.

31

Paige

Dear Rhodes,

~~I'm not dead.~~

Sorry. That was an intense way to start.

I'm stranded.

This isn't the good kind where I can binge a show or book series while eating my weight in Goldfish and Sour Patch Kids. It's the kind where I tell you all of the important things I can't say to your face and may not be able to until I'm home. ~~So, if I die, this is goodbye...~~

Sorry! I'll stop mentioning death.

To my point, I love you.

I love you, Rhodes. I love you so much, I don't know what to do with all of this *feeling*. It's bigger than the volume of my person, and I'm starting to wonder how I've fit it inside of me for so long, lying dormant but still there. Because that's how long I think I've loved you—a long damn time.

It's new and BIGGER than it was, but it's also ravenous like a bear searching for food after a long winter. I was supposed to tell you this before, but here I am, writing it out for you to read too many business days from now. But I can't wait. I can't keep this information inside me any longer.

I love you.

I always have. You know this. But this is the kind of love that has changed. Maybe you're not all that surprised, and maybe I'm not either, because the kind of love we've always had has been built on mutual respect, kindness, and the enjoyment of each other. We were already there in so many ways that matter.

But now, we have an extra layer. An extra dose of love I can't wait to explore.

I love my best friend. I love *you*.

I love how you're the one who can put a smile on my face when I'm grumpy and how you always cover your eyes when I'm changing like the honorable man you are. I love that you drive a small car, touting gas mileage and turning radius in your passionate tirades. I love that you always have treats for Cleo and take a day off to go to the vet with me. I love how you've always been mine but without the label.

How you persisted through every boyfriend or fling I've had is beyond me because now that I've made it to this other side of love, there isn't a chance in hell I could have done it.

I love how much you've loved me.

I'm so ready to start this new phase of our love because you'll always be mine, and I'll always be yours.

Love always,

Paige

32

RHODES

"Have you heard anything?" I stretch all the kinks out of my neck. It doesn't help.

Apparently, stress and sitting in those interconnected airport chairs for a couple of hours will undo all of your hard work at the gym. The metal and pleather combination laughs in the face of muscles.

The airline didn't have any open seats on the earlier flight to Bozeman, so I waited around to board this one, which should be disembarking soon. Not fast enough if you ask me.

"Nothing," Amber says on the other end of the call. "I tried calling the ranger station, too, but they haven't heard of a Paige Turner or any emergencies involving her."

Of course not, because that would be too easy.

I shake my head and rest it on the airplane seat behind me. "And the hotels?"

She sighs, and I know she already regrets telling me before she's said a word. "Nothing there, either."

"Fuck."

"Excuse me, young man!" An older woman with white hair and a hefty-looking purse says. "Watch your language."

"Busted," the voice on the other side of me whispers out the corner of her mouth.

It's the voice of someone who should not be here right now.

The voice I hear in my nightmares.

"Constance, I'm trying to find your sister right now. Would you please stop?"

She gestures at her spot on my other side, closest to the window. "I'm trying to find her, too. That's why I'm here."

Constance was probably the last person I expected to see at my gate before boarding, but after hearing from Amber what was going on, she just showed up without a carry-on or anything else but a black fanny pack the length of my foot. Maybe she's worried like I am. Or maybe she just wants to vacation in Yellowstone. I don't know yet.

I narrow my eyes at her, then turn to the older woman beside me and apologize profusely for my language before Constance makes me deranged, and I get kicked off this plane.

Lowering my voice, I say into my phone: "Keep trying, Amber. Call every place in Yellowstone if you have to, even if it's a gas station. Ask Paige's mom what the van's license plate number is, and maybe they can put the word out at different stations around the park in case they spot her."

"I already described the make and model of the van—*ugly and outdated*—but I'll get the license plate."

"Okay." There's nothing else we can do.

The plane will land late this afternoon, and the earliest I'd get to the park is a couple hours after that. But Yellowstone covers nearly an entire state, miles of land and too many corners. How am I supposed to know where she is?

An idea sparks. "Amber, I have to go."

"Rhodes, be careful—"

I hang up without saying goodbye like all of the Turners do and scroll to my messages with Paige. The last photo she sent is of Cleo on a rock, but the background looks like it's at a rest stop since small vault toilets stand in a linear pattern behind Cleo.

But there's also a waterfall.

"Everyone knows you have to put your phone on airplane mode," Constance says while flipping through the in-flight magazine. "You're probably the only one using yours right now."

She's wearing all-black, her sharp bob cut hovering just beneath her chin makes me think she could actually slice me with the straight edge.

"We haven't even pulled back from the jet bridge." I open a search tab and type: Names of waterfalls in Yellowstone.

Hundreds of matches appear.

So that won't work.

I almost swear out loud again but think better of it if only for the sake of my aching body and the older woman beside me possibly toting bricks in her bag.

"You're not going to find her," Constance states, pausing on a page about available movies. "She's probably dead or in a ditch. Maybe stolen by a family of bears in the woods where she'll meet a modern-day Tarzan who will sweep her off her feet, marry her, and put little wild man babies inside her."

I stare at her, chin nearly touching my chest in awe.

She glances at me, barely turning her head. "What?"

"How could you say that?" I ask, dumbfounded. "Those are all of the worst-case scenarios."

"Exactly." She shrugs. "They're all highly unlikely, but it feels better to get them off my chest. Do you have anything you want to add?"

I keep staring. "No. I don't. And if I did, I'm not letting myself think on them long enough to put the thoughts into words."

She shrugs again and continues reading. "Suit yourself."

My head falls back to the headrest again while I'm caught adding Constance's worst-case scenarios to my own list. Thinking I can somehow find Paige in Yellowstone is a laughable idea now that I'm on a plane to Montana. But I have to at least try. I'm going to drive myself crazy staying home and doing nothing while also not knowing what could be happening or what has happened.

So, here I am.

A helpless man.

No, not just that. I'm a helpless man in a middle seat.

The armrest isn't an option since the older woman who yelled at me hogs it, so I lean to the other side. But Constance stabs me with her pointy elbow.

I'm already tired of fighting with her, so I concede quickly.

I roll my eyes, pulling my elbows into my sides while folding my hands. Thank God this flight is only an hour. I can sit uncomfortably for that long if it means finding Paige at the end of it.

But I don't have that guarantee.

I start my breathing exercises, placing a hand to my stomach to feel it swell with air to ground me in the here and now. *I can't control this.* All I can do is trust and let go. So, I visualize what it will be like to hold Paige in my arms, to see her whole and well as we pull back from the gate and taxi toward the runway. The air above me whistles through the mostly closed vent while the flight attendant shares the details of the in-flight time and weather.

Meanwhile, I'm also forming a plan in my head.

A plan of what the hell I'm going to do in case she's married to Tarzan.

WE LAND IN Bozeman with nothing more than my duffle bag and unrealistic positivity.

And Constance's fanny pack filled to the brim with airline trail mix.

I didn't schedule a rental car pickup, and all of them are booked. Apparently, I'm not the only one planning to visit Yellowstone. So, I had to eat the cost of a rideshare to West Yellowstone for both of us since Constance conveniently forgot everything else in her wallet except for her ID. Where Paige entered is the only thing I know for certain about her travel plans, so it had to be done. Unfortunately, once we arrived, our ride wouldn't take us through the park on an aimless search for the woman I love—ridiculous if you ask me—so we're currently walking on the side of the road.

In Yellowstone.

With Constance, who is about three breaths away from heat stroke. It's nearing evening, but the sun hasn't relented. Wearing all black during summertime was not the right move, but hell if I'll tell her that. Instead, I let her drink all of my water while she munches on bag after bag of trail mix, complaining about how much she wants to murder the sun.

Every time a car passes or I hear a noise, I jump. I'm expecting a bear, a herd of bison, or an elk to take me out before I have a chance to find Paige. Bear spray or one of Machete Lady's knives would've helped. The ranger at the entrance couldn't help us since they were swamped with a line of cars that backed all the way to the light in the small town of West Yellowstone.

So, I just need to find another park ranger who does have the time to help.

I wasn't exactly sure of the rules here, but I threw out my thumb to hitchhike twenty minutes ago. I should have spent more time thinking this through. Hitchhiking our way through this enormous park isn't going to get us far.

"This was a bad idea."

I stop and peer at Constance who is sweating but also still scowling. "I didn't hear you offer any other ideas."

She stops, too. "I had one, but you didn't like it."

"Pretending to be a secret agent and telling the Uber driver *that's classified* to every question he asked convinced him *not* to keep driving us around. It had the opposite effect."

She shrugs. "He doesn't need to know my trip is going. That's creepy."

"You laid it on pretty thick," I state, continuing to walk.

"Stating I have high-level clearance on every continent?" she asks.

"No, the other thing." I can't even say it.

I catch her smirk out of the corner of my eye. "Oh, you mean when I said how easy it is to plant hidden cameras?"

I cringe just hearing her voice it again. It was bad enough catching the very wide, very confused eyes of the driver in the rearview mirror before he kicked us out.

"*That* was creepy," I say, a saltiness brining my words.

"Oops," is all she has to say between bites.

I can't keep walking like this; it's slowing us down. According to the map, the next ranger station isn't too far, less than ten miles, I'm guessing. If we could just get a ride there, I can convince them to do something.

Hooking a thumb, I jut it out toward the road in hopes someone passing by will stop. A few continue on like they don't see me, and I'm okay with that because I barely want to see me. But they have to, I need them to. I flip around and walk backward, hoping to awkwardly make eye contact and guilt someone into stopping. There's no time for pride.

"Put your thumb higher." Constance is still facing forward, elbows to her sides at a ninety-degree angle to accommodate her snacks, and doing nothing to help. "Just so you know," she starts, and I brace for impact while also putting my thumb a little higher in case it helps. "What you're doing for Paige...it's kind of sweet."

Kind of? It's as much of a compliment as I'll probably get. "Thanks."

"Do you, like, love her or something?" she asks, gnashing a pretzel between her teeth with surprising force.

This isn't how I saw this going. Telling Paige's sister how I feel before I get a chance to tell Paige again, but I have nothing to hide. My actions have already been fairly obvious. "I do. A lot. For a long time now."

Constance considers this while staring forward blankly. "I know."

I scoff and shake my head as another car passes. "Then why'd you ask?"

"Because," she begins, "you needed to say it out loud. And it's why I'm here."

I swing my gaze to her. "And why is that?"

"So you'll go through with it," she says simply. "If you hadn't noticed, my sister is...in her head a lot. Sometimes, you need to chase her to remind her you aren't going anywhere."

What she says makes a lot of sense. Paige likes to run, but it's also because she's had to survive by jumping from one job to the next along with every boyfriends who have left her without a backward glance. But I don't have time to respond because someone slows down and pulls to the shoulder.

I swat Constance on her shoulder, and she dramatically flails her body as though I've hit her. "Yes, sir," she says under her breath with a laugh that is barely concealed.

"Please don't ruin this," I say with a whine since I can't help it. "It's the first and only car that has stopped."

She stands to her full height and tucks the empty snack bag into her fanny pack. "Just trying to make this more interesting for you so when you finally do find her, it's worth it."

"It'll be worth it regardless."

We don't have time to keep sniping back and forth since the woman in the passenger seat rolls down her window. "Where ya headed?"

A part of me wishes I would have been more particular about which cars I put my hand out for. This one looks like a Chevy Spark, but all of the identifiers, such as a hood ornament, are gone. It's packed to the roof, and then there are more things strapped onto the top, albeit not very securely.

"We…" I hesitate, wondering if I should let Constance scare them off. Fuck it. "We need to get to the next ranger station. Should be just over ten miles. Do you have room for two?"

"We can take them there, right, Richard?" Her honey-sweet voice is as convincing as that blonde hair of hers.

A grunt is his only response, but she squeals, so I suppose that's a *yes*.

"Hop on in next to little Timmy and Babi," she says with a smile. "Oh, and Clementine. Don't worry, she doesn't bite."

The Golden Retriever currently sitting between the two children, who are somewhere between eight and ten years old, looks as if she's being held against her will. The overactive eyebrows and shifting gaze scream *beware*, but we don't have the luxury of waiting, so I gesture for Constance to get in first.

"Hold on." She slams a flat palm to my chest. "I should do a sweep of the vehicle first."

I glare at her. "It's fine."

Little Timmy lets me have the window seat, which really isn't that much better since my head still has to bend to fit inside. Clementine is sitting on his lap now with her front paws on mine, and Constance is sitting by the other window with Babi sandwiched between us.

Clementine looks up at me, mouth open and panting as a large glob of drool lands on my leg.

"I'm Frida," the woman in front says, turning to look at us. "We'll get you to where you need to be."

Constance lowers her voice. "Do you have any dog treats?"

"Why, of course I do!" Frida eagerly whips out a bag of treats and hands one to Constance, who I'm assuming is going to give it to Clementine.

Instead, she surprises me and puts it in my mouth, patting my head. "Good husband."

Frida shrieks with laughter. "You two are just the cutest!"

I spit the treat out, Clementine diving between my legs for it, and glare at Constance again, speaking through my tight lips. "What are you doing?"

She lowers her voice to a whisper, "Treating you like the Golden Retriever you are and making this believable."

"How is this—"

Little Timmy pats my head, which he has to reach for. "Good boy."

Constance's smile is so broad it nearly reveals the teeth I've barely seen right as Frida turns to wink at us while her husband pulls back onto the two-lane road.

It doesn't assure me in the slightest.

33

Paige

I wake up to someone pounding on my window.

Okay, *knocking*, but it woke me from a dead sleep, so it sounded more aggressive. The clock on the counter is a dirty liar because it says six p.m. There's no way I napped for three hours.

But as I sit up and push the curtain aside, I realize the sun is waning in the sky, getting ready to drop below the mountainscape.

Whoever is outside knocks again.

Glad to know my stress nap worked, except now I'm stressed again at the realization I'm still in a shit ton of trouble. I moan but drag myself out of Cleocatra's warm embrace.

"Coming!" I yell, looking for a weapon I can use in case the person outside has ill intentions.

A pair of tongs is the closest I can come up with on short notice, so I arm myself with them and walk to the door. The van is hot now since the AC is no longer running, and the windows are foggy enough I can only make out a shape, not a face.

I take a deep breath and peer at Cleo, nodding. She's got my back in case anything goes wrong.

Flinging open the door, I don't bother with *hello* or *how can I help you*. I go straight for, "I'm armed!"

The man staring back at me is the last person I expected to see, but my heart swells seeing him.

"You came."

His large-brimmed hat holds the familiar Yellowstone National Park crest, and he's wearing dark green pants with a matching shirt. The large backpack sticking up well above his head has me feeling instantly relieved he's here to save me.

"Evening, ma'am," he says, clearing his throat and hiking his pack higher. "I was hoping you had some water. I lost my water bottle some ways back, and I still have quite a bit of road left to travel."

My face falls. "You aren't a ranger?"

He shakes his head with a creased brow. "I'm Jeff from Utah. Just here to hike."

Well, thanks a lot Jeff from Utah.

I nod slowly, realizing a ranger likely wouldn't stop unless my car had been here for days. Plenty of people like this man pull off to the side of the road to venture out into the woods. The booklet said there were tons of marked trails throughout the park.

"Oh." I lower the tongs, hiding them behind my back in case there's a chance he didn't see them already. "Hang on a minute."

He nods and steps back as I shut the door. I only have two water bottles, but I need to keep one for myself. The one I grab is a plastic one I got at Upstairs Closet Thrift a few months ago with a cracked lid. The bottle doesn't leak, so it should be fine for him. I fill it up from the sink after flipping the switch on my water tank.

I'm capping the bottle when I hear a scuffle outside.

"Who are you? What the fuck are you doing here?" another voice says.

My eyes widen, and I rush to the door, flinging it open without a second thought. Just as I do, I hear the guy who asked for water start to say: "I'm just getting water—"

A figure barrels forward in a dark sweatshirt, forcing Jeff from Utah to walk backward. "This isn't a store. Go find somewhere else to get water!"

"Rhodes?"

Oh shit.

He whips around, eyes a little wild, hair even more so. "Paige."

I look to Jeff from Utah, who is no threat to society like Rhodes wants to believe.

"He was trying to take advantage of you," Rhodes says, carelessly pointing at him while walking closer to me. "Are you okay? Are you hurt?"

"I was not!" Jeff from Utah retorts.

"I'm fine." I nod and extend the water bottle to the guy. "Sorry about that."

He peers between Rhodes and the bottle, deciding he's okay to grab it, so he does. It's fast, and he turns around immediately to stalk off, looking back over his shoulder. "Thank you again."

Rhodes waves. "Sorry."

Our gazes lock once more. It's so shocking to see him standing in front of me, acting like a big macho hero coming to save his princess from the fire-breathing dragons guarding the tower. Okay, it's actually pretty great and very different. Yellowstone doesn't have dragons. But there are some similar aspects, like the fact he's *here*.

"What are you—"

I'm cut off when he steps forward, pulling me out of the open door at my waist and pinning me to the side of the van. This is nothing like the near punch he almost threw at a stranger. This is a man who is *hungry*.

He cradles my face in his hands. "You have three seconds to tell me you either need to go to the hospital or you don't want me to kiss you."

"I don't need a hospital." But maybe I do based on how quickly my heart is galloping outside my body.

It's enough for him since he tilts my face up and kisses me.

This isn't a made-for-TV kind of kiss, either. His tongue is in my mouth, hands diving into my sleep-mussed hair. It's urgent and insistent as he pushes closer until there isn't a breath of space between us and I'm flat against the van. His hips hold me in place even though I'm not a flight risk. In fact, there's no other place I'd rather be.

My brain finally catches up, and I kiss him back, matching his intensity and the relief coursing through me that he's *here*. The press of his mouth on mine softens, and his kisses become almost languid like we're swimming in a pool of oil.

"Woo!" someone else calls. "Guess you found what you were looking for."

Rhodes pulls away even though I'm gripping handfuls of his sweatshirt, trying to keep him close. His lips are red, and he's breathing heavily.

I've already forgotten about the other voices, but he hasn't. He turns to look at them, giving a small wave. "Thanks for the ride!"

Quickly cataloging the small vehicle with multiple humans inside *and* a dog, I can't decipher where he ever fit. "Did you drive all the way here with them?" My brain finally registers that he got here somehow and who else is in the car. "Constance?"

Constance salutes me while the dog sits directly on her lap, head out the window.

"No, we rode with them through the park," Rhodes says. "And Constance surprised me at the airport. We were just on our way to the ranger station when I saw your van."

"Did you tell her yet?" Constance yells at Rhodes.

I crane my neck to look at him. "Tell me what?"

"Later," he whispers to me, then hollers, "Get lost, Constance!"

"I plan to," she calls back. "Onward, weird family!" she shouts.

"Need anything else before we take off?" the woman with bleach-blonde hair asks. "Your wife?"

Wife?

Rhodes replies with a quick, "We're good," while I scream, "Yes!"

He looks at me, and I shrug sheepishly. "I'm out of gas."

"How—" He stops himself. "Nevermind. Do you have the empty gas can I packed you?"

"You packed me a gas can?" I feel him pull away, stepping back, and I don't like it. I don't want to talk about gas cans or safety. I want to keep kissing.

My brain is still so immersed in the conversation our mouths were just having.

But we have problems to fix.

Rhodes drops his hands from my waist but tugs me by the hand to the back of the van where he opens both doors to rummage through a few things. He hoists the gas can up when he finds it.

Turning to the blonde woman still hanging out her car, he asks: "Can we get a ride to fill this?"

"Hop in you two lovebirds!" She beams and waves us over. "This must be your mistress."

I have no idea what's happening.

Rhodes scratches the back of his neck while I grab the door handle. "Uh, yeah. Something like that."

I narrow my eyes at him, and he widens his, begging me to just go with it.

Constance hugs the dog on her lap, who is easily heavier than her, and address me. "You're alive!"

"I'm alive," I say, less enthusiastically. "What are you doing here?"

The two children scoot over to make room for us.

"Grand gesturing you."

I wrinkle my brow as Rhodes tugs me closer before I can slide in. "FYI, they have a dog, and it will probably drool on you."

I nod before realizing Cleo is still in the van. My head is in another realm. "Hold on." I squeeze his hand, then let it drop. "I'll be right back."

I jog to the van's side door and swing it open, snatching the harness, leash, and Cleo. Back outside, I clutch her closer to my chest as she tries to leap free.

"Any chance we have room for one more?"

The woman nods. "Clementine is great with cats."

34

CLEOCATRA

I am utterly appalled they made me breathe the same air as that panting low-life they call a *dog*.

It had no manners, staring at me and drooling.

Gross.

Have some self-respect.

Dad's shoulder will now bear the marks of my displeasure. But only a little because I'm still glad he came. I was starting to worry we'd be forced to live outside. *Forever.* I'm a house cat at my core. My paws are not built for dirt or manual labor.

35

Paige

On our way back from filling the gas can, Frida decides to play some Dolly Parton, which seems to make everyone in the car more lively than when we first crawled in.

Cleo curled around Rhodes' shoulders, avoiding Clementine like she had an incurable disease—I suppose being a dog fits that bill. I'm partially sitting on Rhodes' lap while Timmy and Babi squish toward the other side of the car, and Constance sits in the middle with Clementine on her lap.

The man driving hasn't said one word and has to roll down the windows when our collective breathing starts fogging them up.

I lean into Rhodes, still in astonishment he's here while also relishing how solid and real he feels. I try to speak quieter than Dolly's chorus. "I take back everything I said about your car being small."

"I accept."

Feeling eyes on me, I peer to my side. Clementine is still staring. "Is she looking at me or you?"

"Both of us?" Rhodes rests a hand on my thigh. "No, you know what, she's probably watching Cleo."

Cleo might be staying clear of Clementine's jump radius, but that doesn't mean she hasn't taunted her with a swishing tail and low growl.

She is petty, after all. Clementine whines at the back of her throat but doesn't take the bait.

My van comes into view once again, and I sigh with relief—but not too much, because breathing in this cramped space is hard.

"Did you text Amber and my parents back, by the way?" I hate knowing everyone was so worried about me while I was napping and eating orange slices.

Rhodes nods. "She alerted your parents, Machete Lady, and the media that you are indeed alive."

"The media?" I question.

He shrugs. "You know how Amber is when she's worried."

I do because it wouldn't have been the first time I've scared her like this. Once, she even had the cops swing by my house for a wellness check. I was just reupholstering a chair and hadn't looked at my phone in hours.

"Well," I start when the car comes to a stop. "Thank you so much for driving us to the gas station. I really appreciate it."

"You are so welcome, darlin'," Frida says, and the man driving grumbles. For every one hundred words she speaks, her husband says negative ten. "I'm so glad y'all found each other."

I nod my head. "Me, too."

There is still so much to talk about, to explain.

But there isn't time for that since Frida adds, "Your love triangle is inspiring."

I peer over at Constance, who has been tapping the beat of every Dolly Parton song on Clementine's back. *How does she know every song?* I could have sworn I heard a few lyrics fall from her mouth as well.

Constance gives some sort of fake laugh that is far too loud and nowhere near her real one. "Frida, dear, everyone knows squares are better!"

Rhodes whispers in my ear, "I prefer rectangles."

The memory of a time when I thought my best friend was someone else and I described my body type to him comes back, making my face flush with heat.

Frida's brows crinkle like she's confused by all of the shape talk.

When they park in front of Vincent VanGo, Rhodes pulls Cleo from his shoulders, her claws fully extended and clinging to his T-shirt as though she'll never release him. He offers me a hand and then Constance.

But Constance shakes her head, a sly grin tugging at her lips as she and Rhodes have a conversation between their eyes.

He slams the door, and Frida cranes out the window. "What about your wife?"

Rhodes keeps smiling at Constance. "You can keep her."

We wave politely until the family is out of sight, Constance joining their fun, at least for now, and I can finally breathe.

Except when I look at Rhodes, then I can't.

There's a steadiness to his gaze that's new and unrelenting. I tug at the hem of my T-shirt, if only because he makes me feel more exposed. He's seen me half-naked, and we've admitted things to each other. New and exciting things that are also vague and open-ended because there is so much time in our future for me to screw this up.

"Where'd you go?" he asks, setting the gas can down by the front tire without looking away. "You're chewing on your bottom lip, and your color is washed out."

I sink my hands into the back pockets of my jean shorts. "What do you mean? I'm always pale."

He quirks his head to the side. "Are you worried about something?"

Just the quality and longevity of life for this new relationship of ours. "No."

He shifts on his feet, holding Cleo against his chest with one arm. "Paige."

"What?" I turn and open the van door. "It's nothing."

He walks around me to put Cleo inside the van, but he doesn't go in or retrieve the gas can to get us out of this bind. He shuts the door and watches me.

I squirm. "This feels new."

"It does," he agrees but waits for me to continue.

Another car passes by, and I can only wonder what they think is happening right now between us. I barely know.

I exhale and peer up at him, even if my eye contact is dodgy. "What if I mess this up?" The truth rolls off my tongue easily, but it still shocks me. "I...I don't want to. But my history isn't exactly stellar."

"I'm aware." He gives me a cheeky grin.

I turn my attention to the packed earth under my feet that's slightly dampened and littered with rocks, leaves, twigs, and bits of trash I promise myself to pick up later. It's chilly out, and goosebumps rise on my arms and legs.

He notices and steps closer. "I can't look into the future and know what will happen." *That's unfortunate.* "But we're here now. You're safe. And I'm committed."

I'm committed.

Those two words jilt my heart as he says them. They are like finally remembering the combination to your bike lock after forgetting or finding leftovers in your fridge from the night before that you thought were long gone.

It's excitement mixed with a kind of relief I haven't felt this whole trip. It's as if The Itch inside me quiets down enough to hear him out.

"Thank you." My voice is barely audible.

He extends his hand for me to take and pulls me to him. He bends, nuzzling his nose into the base of my neck and inhaling deeply. "We are in this together now. With all of our messy."

Tears perch on my eyelids as I sink further into his chest, relishing the familiar scent of my best friend, who is also more. So much more.

Minutes pass before either of us makes a move or says anything. But when he finally does, his words are low, an invitation.

"We could fill the gas up later," he suggests.

"We could."

"Are you hungry?"

I shake my head against his firm body.

"Do you need anything?"

Just you, my mind wants to say, but I hold back. Not because I don't think he'd appreciate it, but because I'm still treading carefully. I want to climb this man so fast, but I've already tried rushing it. What if he isn't ready? What if he still wants to wait?

"Nothing," I say, nuzzling closer.

Circling his arms around my waist tighter, he steps us back until I'm against the side passenger door. "Are you sure?"

I swallow, tipping my head up to stare into his lowered gaze. "I'm positive."

He slowly leans closer, giving me every chance to escape, to turn and do something else I've already told him I don't need to do right now.

I don't move.

His pace is slow, drawing out every desire from my body in the multitude of seconds it takes for his lips to touch mine.

"Rhodes," I say, his lips hovering close.

One hand caresses my cheek, dropping lower until he's cradling the back of my neck and tentatively touching his mouth to mine again. The way my body turns to liquid fire, pooling in too many places as he drags his lips over my wet ones, is welcome. Suddenly, I have so many needs for someone who said they had none.

I need him to touch me.

I need him to hold my body upright.

I need him to get closer.

"You're here," I whisper, solidifying everything he went through to be here.

He nods, teasing my lips with gentle brushes before knocking his nose to mine and gingerly pushing the bridge of my glasses up my nose. "I couldn't get a hold of you."

I roll my eyes at the absurdity and smile. "One of the bison decided to get a little rough, bumping into my van. Since my window wouldn't roll up, the next thing I knew, my phone was flying out. The beast and all her friends stepped on it."

I sound insane trying to recount the story, but he doesn't think twice.

"So, your phone broke," he confirms, and I nod. "And it was a bison, not Tarzan?"

My eyes go wide. "Tarzan?"

"Never mind."

"Is that why you almost hurt that man?" Everything becomes more transparent.

"I kind of lost it on that guy, thinking maybe he would hurt you." He runs a thumb down my cheek.

"I'm okay," I tell him.

"I can see that."

A smile lifts my mouth. "So you flew out here, drove to Yellowstone, and found a ride through the park just to come find me?"

He laughs a little and rubs the back of his neck, other hand content to trace my hip bone. "I guess I did." His cheeks redden. "I wasn't trying to crash your trip. But hearing you scream...the way you asked for help...I couldn't just ignore that. I had to make sure you were okay. I'll always be there for you."

There are so many questions in my head I want to ask, but all of them pale in comparison to being here with him now. He came for me. He traveled a good distance with my sister, just for me. I don't want to waste another second asking when, in reality, I already know the answer I really need.

I forcefully push to my tiptoes and kiss him again.

He has to grab me since the brunt with which I leapt at him was more than he was expecting. But he easily settles one hand on my lower back while the other caresses my face, tracing the fuse of our mouths as they move against each other. I can't get enough of his taste, this kiss, this man I'm so gone for.

It feels like we've wasted time. Like maybe we should have been doing this all along. We should have been kissing, hugging, being with one another. Two states later, and I'm just now starting to see what Rhodes saw all along.

And he never gave up on me.

This thought sparks a new rush of emotions that hijack my body.

"You came for me," I say out loud between kisses.

"I did." His hand slides to cup my ass, putting space between my back and the van.

I pull back enough to search his eyes. "You always do; you always have."

He nods. "I always will."

My expression softens, but the coil winding in my body tightens. It's like my heart has been released to love this man fully, and I'm helpless to do anything but.

36

RHODES

Paige above me, hair tickling my face while she stares at my lips, is the best damn vision I can think of.

Except it isn't a vision.

It's real.

My very real hands on her very real hips are a testament to that.

After becoming breathless from our kiss outside, we moved inside the van, where she pushed me back on the bed. I hit my head on the ceiling vent, but it was quickly forgotten when she came down on top of me. The press of her body distracted me completely.

My hands wander over her pliant body as her lips tenderly drop to mine once more. I inhale through my nose, elated this is finally happening—I'm kissing Paige—but also worried it's a mirage I've somehow conjured up. Maybe I'm still walking on the side of the road right now. Maybe it's not really her hips filling my palms or her breasts rubbing against my chest.

But when I open my eyes, she's still there. Still looking at me with those big, brown eyes of hers, thinking the same thing I am. I'd bet on it.

"We're really doing this," I find myself saying.

She laughs against my mouth and pushes up to straight arms, her hips now creating more pressure on my groin. Instinct tells me to roll my hips, seek out the friction I'm desperate for, but I wait, watching for what she says or does next. I don't want to push her further than she wants to go.

Everything is so new, fragile still.

But Paige surprises me and sits fully on my lap, lifting the hem of her shirt above her head. Her light blue bralette has a lace edging along the top that is begging for my hands and mouth.

I lick my lips. I've seen her in her bra plenty of times. I've always forced myself to look away quickly, keeping the friendship between us firmly in place. But here, it's an invitation—a welcome home banner after a long trip away.

"Can I touch you?" I grind out.

She smirks down at me. "Please."

She starts to move her hips, rocking them as she uses the roof of the van to brace herself and keep steady.

My hands are everywhere. Climbing her rippling stomach, teasing the underside of this sexy little bra, and feeling the soft ribbing covering her as I run my thumb across her nipples. The soft moan she makes elicits so much, it has me lifting my hips to meet hers and rubbing circles around her peaks.

"I never thought we'd be here," she says on an exhale. "I don't know why. It makes so much sense. You and me. We work."

We do work.

She rides me, my jeans becoming unbearably tight while her shorts ride higher. I brace my hands on her thighs, feeling the soft heat of her skin and wishing I could somehow be closer. All over her, inside her.

Bowing her head, her kiss is erratic and so fucking hot, it corners my brain. My hands skate up her back to find the clasp to her bra, but there isn't one.

"It lifts over my head," she says, sitting up and raising her arms again in invitation.

Instead of taking her bra off like this, I flip her to the mattress and push to hover over her. Unfortunately, the wall is closer than I guessed, so I smack my elbow into it, causing the pain to reverberate up my arm.

"I'm okay," I say quickly to assure her, though my pride is stinging a bit.

"Swear?" she asks, brows diving in concern.

"Swear."

Her arms stretch higher above her head, resting on the soft mattress beneath her as I drag my fingers up her sides until they're under the elastic stretching across her ribs again, pushing slowly and lifting to release her perfect breasts.

My mouth gapes, and so does hers, but I might be the only one breathless.

The sight beneath me is better than my imagination or any photo. The pink skin of her nipple against her porcelain, cream-colored skin is so alluring. I'm trying my hardest to hold myself up while I lift the rest of her bra over her head and take her into my hands. I lean down and slowly kiss her, licking down her neck and collarbone to her sensitive nipple with lazy movements. I'm taking my time and frustrating her in the process.

"If you don't put your full mouth on me in a second, I'm going to do it for you," she demands.

I smile up at her, smirking as I tease. "I've waited a long time for this. I'm not going to rush it."

"We have a lot of time, though," she complains. "Right now, I just need you. I need us. I need..." Her breath hitches as I pull her into my mouth, swirling my tongue around her nipple. "That."

She grips handfuls of my hair, pressing me closer as if I weren't already there, and squirming underneath my body as I pin her down and keep her from floating away. The moans at the back of her throat are louder now, and I let go of her breast and take her mouth instead.

Her kisses are still urgent, prodding me further along until we're both panting, biting, and licking one another like we've been doing it for centuries. The pressure in my pants is pushing further into her leg, and her hips are seeking for the firm strain in my pants I'm so damn willing to offer.

"I want you, Paige. So badly. So desperately," I say when she wraps her ankles around my back, allowing me deeper between her legs.

I close my eyes at how good she feels curled around me like this, but how much better it will feel when I'm inside her. I pump my hips as I kiss her. Harder until I'm so stiff, so in need, that I have to pause.

I roll off her to my side so I don't end this moment too soon.

"Where are you going?" she asks.

I cup her face, then adjust myself in my jeans. "Nowhere. I just need a sec."

"Rhodes," she says, drawing out my name. "You should have said something."

I study her expression, but her hands are quick, reaching for the button on my jeans and rendering me speechless.

My zipper goes next, easily becoming the loudest noise in this confined space. Her hand dives into the side of my boxers, not even touching me yet—only my hip—but I take a sharp inhale and brace for the moment.

The moment she scatters my thoughts.

The moment I will beg for if I have to.

The moment I make her *mine*.

She goes back to teasing the elastic band at my waist with her finger before her hand circles around me, pumping slowly like I teased her nipples, lips crashing and sucking. I grab the back of her head and hold her to me. Small gasps leave my mouth when she reaches my tip with her thumb.

Rolling over her, I pin her hands above her head with one hand while I use the other to prop myself up. "You can't keep doing that."

She smirks. "Why not, Rhodes?"

"You know why."

She's breathing hard through her nose, closing her eyes. "Then do whatever you have to do to help me with this ache."

I release her hands and then roll over to my side again to kick off my jeans faster than I ever have before. Taking my shirt off when the ceiling encroaches on my head is difficult, but I use my abs to hold me up and yank it off.

My mouth is back on the delicious skin at her neck, kissing hard and nibbling at the base where she tastes so sweet, I can't think straight. I'm on her breasts next, licking around each nipple before pressing light pecks to her stomach. It ripples as I kiss and lick my way to the button of her shorts. I breathe lightly on her stomach, tickling her enough that she yanks at my shoulders.

"This probably isn't the right time to tell you this," she says, concern on her face as I hover above her.

I sober immediately. "What? Is something wrong? Are you okay?"

We're both panting hard, struggling to take in a full breath of air. "I'm fine. Everything's…fine. I just don't have a condom."

Realization sparks. "Not one?"

She pushes up to her elbows, bites her lower lip, and shakes her head.

My palm is still firmly planted on her stomach while watching the rise and fall of those perfect—

Think, Rhodes!

"Okay. I don't have one either." Making love to Paige in the back of her van while flashing Cleo some ass cheek wasn't exactly on my mind when I was rushing here to make sure she was safe. "And I know you're not on birth control."

"Wait a second...." Her pointer finger finds the middle of my forehead and pushes. "How do you know that?"

I pretend to bite her finger. "Because you and Amber talk about your cycles all the time when I'm around. She's on birth control because of her intense cramps, but you're not because you don't like how it makes you feel crazy."

She's stunned. "You remembered all of that?"

My expression softens as I trace patterns on her stomach, connecting freckles like I've only done in my mind. "I don't forget when it comes to you." I exhale through my nose. "I remember how you like your eggs—scrambled with ketchup. How you can't go to the movies without the sour gummy candy that you always sneak in because, according to you, *the prices at the theater are outrageous*. I know you take an 'everything' shower each Sunday night and never fold any of your laundry."

"You..." Her words trail off, and her mouth goes slack. I can see the tears welling in her eyes again, and I instinctively raise a hand to graze her cheek. "Noticed."

"Of course I did. I've been noticing you for a long time." I catch the lonesome tear that streaks down her face. "And I don't want to stop. I want to know how you sound when you come undone. Become familiar with every gasp you make, or when you hold your breath when I do this..." I swirl the tip of my tongue around her belly button, eliciting a slight moan at the top of her inhale. "I want to get to know these parts of you, too."

"I want to figure them out with you." She cradles my cheek. "But what about a condom?"

I let my hand track down her neck, grazing the soft skin between her breasts, and then lower down her stomach. My eyes are locked on hers as I finger the button on her jeans and slide the zipper down.

"It's your birthday." Looking briefly at the underwear she's wearing, purely out of my own curiosity, I tease the elastic just like she did with mine. "It doesn't mean we can't do other things."

The elastic snaps back, and I push off the bed until my feet are heavy on the floor. She stays propped on her elbows, and I try to stay focused on the jean shorts I'm ready to rip off her when her tits are right there, begging me to change my mind.

I lightly push her shoulders back onto the bed, giving each breast a temporary squeeze before dragging rough hands down her sides to her shorts. I tug them off as she wiggles her hips to help, and just like that, they're gone. *Just like that.* I can't help lowering my mouth to the cursive font on the front of her underwear reading *Tuesday*. It's actually Sunday, but it still makes me smile.

My breath is hot against the thin cotton, forcing me to dig my fingers deeper into her hips before shoving her knees up to the ceiling. I lower to my knees, which still makes me tall enough to reach the warmth between her legs. I drag a finger down her center and listen to her sigh. It's the perfect sound; all I can think about is her and giving her everything she wants.

"Tell me everything. What you like, what you don't, everything. Okay?"

"Okay," she all but whispers.

I tug on her panties, baring her to the coolness of the van as I slip them off her feet. I immediately bring my mouth to her. She gasps and shudders at the first touch of my tongue, and I give her a chance to adjust by blowing on the sensitive nerves of her clit.

"That. I've never...it's so good. So erotic." Goosebumps erupt on her skin, down her legs and calves, so I drag my hands up the sides, cradling the outside of her thighs as I reverently devour this woman with my mouth.

She tangles one hand in my hair, gripping and tugging. Not away, but closer. My nose knocks against her clit then I lick and kiss and toy with her folds. She's perfect in how she moans, how she rocks against my face as my tongue moves faster, and how her thighs clench the sides of my head to hold me steady.

"All of this. Don't you dare stop," she manages to say.

I wouldn't dare.

My cock is rock solid, and as her noises shift, becoming louder, more strangled, wild even, I reach into my boxers with one hand and stroke myself to the beat of her moans of pleasure. It doesn't take much to pull her over the edge, and I'm right behind her as my hand moves faster up and down my shaft. I keep my mouth on her as she rides out her orgasm, and then I come apart.

Shattering at her feet, I breathe hard against her skin, turning my head to bite the inside of her thigh. Her hands are still in my hair as we both come down from the high of each other.

Since I'm already in the kitchen—the benefits of a tight space—I reach for the dish towel hanging off one of the cabinet hooks and clean us both up.

"You didn't have to do that," I believe she says since her words are muffled and distant.

"I don't have to do a lot of things."

She props herself up on her elbows, completely comfortable with how perfectly naked she is. "Like fly to Montana to come find me?"

"Technically," I start, pulling up my boxers. "I'm in Wyoming now."

"Semantics."

I laugh. "How do you think people who live in Wyoming will feel?"

"You've barely even seen the state," she retorts.

"You're right." I don't bother putting my jeans on because if I have any say, we'll be doing this again as soon as possible. "I've been too busy looking at you."

"And for me."

"That too." I smile while crawling into bed to lay next to her, my feet dangling off the edge as I push a few stray hairs out of her face.

"Why doesn't this feel weird?" she whispers, curling to her side without reaching for the blankets.

Satiated and thoroughly kissed, there's a lightness to her features now. "I think some would say it's because we started as friends. They might also say it's because we already kissed."

She props her head on her hand. "I don't care what *some* say. I want to know what you think."

"I'd say..." For the past few seconds, I've been tracing her cupid's bow with my gaze, so I let my finger do it now, lingering on the truly delectable freckle above her top lip. "All of those things are true. But I'd also add that we've always been each other's safe place. Being physically vulnerable is just another addition to what's already true."

She smiles, and it lifts her entire face. "I like that answer."

I lean forward and kiss her softly, savoring the feel and taste of her lips. How perfect they are for *me*.

"Take me home, would ya?" She pulls me in close, taking my kiss and tripling it.

I have zero complaints.

37

Cleocatra

This is my naptime.

The noises they are making are wholly undignified and far too loud for my liking. Sleep escapes me, so I'm forced to stare off in the opposite direction.

Now my neck hurts.

And I'm hungry.

Maybe they need a reminder it is time for me to eat.

A loud, imposing reminder that involves jumping on the bed and awkwardly staring at them until they do something about it.

Yes. I like this plan.

I will do this.

38

Paige

I couldn't have asked for a better trip to Yellowstone.

Mainly because Rhodes was with me to experience it.

We drove to Yellowstone Lake to stay at the campground I booked for a night, exploring and hiking nearby. Last night, he cooked me hot dogs and macaroni over my single burner camp stove because it's all the small convenience store had when we stopped to see the Old Faithful geyser.

We fell asleep that night after he stole my breath with another visit between my thighs. When I continued to hear very suspicious noises outside, he got up to check every lock on the door, pet Cleo who refused to leave her cat bed, and climbed back in bed with me. He pulled my back to his chest and massaged my arm, shoulder, and hip until I was crawling on top of him again.

I forgot all about the noises.

This morning, I made us cereal—okay, prepared—before we took off in the van.

On our way to the Lamar Valley, we saw a mama bear and her two cubs climbing an embankment near the road. The cars in front of us totally missed them, and Rhodes almost did, too, but my scream helped.

They were adorable and utterly unimpressed with us, thankfully.

Later that afternoon, after seeing the largest bison herd in the valley, we circled our way back to Mammoth Hot Springs around dinner time. There weren't as many people on the winding wood plank pathways leading to the top, giving us ample room to play tag like we were kids again. I won since I bent him backward over a visitor sign to get him and then thoroughly distracted him with our hundredth kiss in an hour.

He held my hand the entire way down, pulling me in to steal kisses and remind me exactly what he could do with that mouth of his. I'm a wanting mess by the time we reach the small parking lot.

"Should we go to the visitor's center?" he asks, starting up the van.

I buckle in and shake my head. "I want to go to our next spot. Now."

His smile lifts, then turns into a sly grin. "Where to?"

I smile, knowing he's going to love this. "Thirst Trapp Farms."

He peers at me as we head through the small town of Mammoth toward the park's North entrance in Gardiner. "Say that again."

"Thirst Trapp Farms."

He gives me a questioning look.

"I found them on social media a couple days ago and booked it on Experiences R Us. It's a working farm that has cabins to stay in, but they also added a few water and electric hookups for vans or RVs," I explain. "There are also things you can do there like horseback riding, cow hugging, hiking, etc."

"Sounds like an adventure." He steals my hand from my lap even if he has to reach across the wide cavern between our seats to do it.

Wait until he sees what kinds of adventures they have there.

"What about Constance? Is she meeting up with us today?" I ask him.

"She texted this morning saying that family is driving her to the airport on their way to Norris Hot Springs."

"They're what?" My sister has lost her mind.

I almost didn't believe her yesterday when I used Rhodes' phone to call her. She apparently agreed to continue traveling with them until I realized this family put her up in her own hotel room after giving them a sob story about her husband running off with his mistress after he stole her wallet.

I don't know how we're related.

"Don't ask me," he says. "Constance lives in a realm I've never visited."

We both laugh, and I ask, "How'd she get a ticket home if her husband—*ex*-husband—stole her wallet?"

"Your Mom and Dad, I'm sure."

I shake my head at this, wanting to call my parents and tell them to stop picking up her messes, but I don't because boundaries exist inside me now. They need to figure out their own stuff.

Rhodes' eyes are on the road, shaking his head when I peer over. The sharp line of his jaw is covered in a five o'clock shadow that would likely knick my fingers if I traced it. The inside of my thighs are already marked with a slight rash because of it. I not so secretly love it. And some of his hair falls over his forehead despite his multiple attempts to push it back; finger tracks run through the rest of his hair.

"Rhodes." I startle us both.

He looks at me with those two hazel eyes that sometimes have gold flecks and other times look more green. "Yeah?"

"What happens now?"

He doesn't answer the literal version of my question with *we're going to grab dinner* or *we're driving to that farm*. No. Instead, he answers the other twenty questions behind this one.

"I'm going to ask you to be my girlfriend, and then we're never going to get enough of each other even though we'll try our damndest every day. We're going to spend time with each other like we did before, but it will probably involve more kissing..." he swings his gaze to me, "and other things. We'll have dinner at your family's house, sometimes mine, and you can stay over at my place since Constance will likely torment both of us if we stay at yours."

I laugh because he's absolutely right about all of this.

"We'll live our lives...together."

I lean my head back and keep looking at him, studying the ways his love shows up on his face. "I like the sound of all that."

He squeezes my hand.

He's already looking back at the road and doesn't see my smile drop. "And what about my career? My livelihood? What am I supposed to do about that?"

"Whatever you want."

I shake my head and then look forward. "What if it isn't in Washington?"

He's quiet for a beat. "Then we don't live in Washington."

"We?"

He looks at me for longer stretches while navigating the many turns in front of us. "Paige, yes. I'm in this now. Together. With you. There isn't another person I want to spend forever with. I would put a ring on your finger today, put a baby inside you, move to Timbuktu, or live in your parent's basement. I would do any of it as long as we're doing it together."

I swallow the lump in my throat that rises at his words. "You'd do that?"

"Yes."

No hesitation, just one word that sends pure fire through me. He doesn't have to do this. We could start off slow or maybe backtrack a little since we've already jumped pretty far in this short span of time. But he doesn't seem bothered by that. He isn't afraid of commitment like some of my other boyfriends were. He's sure about me, and that changes everything.

He is what my heart has needed.

"Pull over."

He double-takes. "What?"

"Pull the van over."

He must see something in my steely gaze because he does what I say. The van isn't fully in park before I'm climbing out of my seat and into his lap. I honk the horn with my ass, but the seat is already pushed back as far as it can go because of his long legs.

I cradle his face with my hands. "I want forever with you, too."

He frames my hips with his hands and tugs me closer over his lap. "I'll do whatever I have to in order to keep you in my life. If that means being friends with you until my last breath, I'd do it. But if it means having you in my bed—since yours is much shorter than mine—holding you whenever I want, kissing you..." he shakes his head, "I won't ask for anything more in my whole life as long as I get this—*you*."

My mouth crushes against his, swallowing the *you* he barely finished saying. I kiss him with all of the heat and pressure that has built in my body. With teeth and frantic hands. It's my fingers scraping through his hair this time, tugging him closer as he makes a mess out of me yet again. But I don't care. I prefer it. I crave being undone like this with him because he was right: he's my safe place. The man who somehow makes me feel protected from miles away, who would travel by pack mule, Chevy Spark, or skateboard to get to me.

"I love you so much, Rhodes." My confession is spoken between hip rolls and clashing tongues, but I want him to hear it, so I say it again, louder this time. "I love you."

"God, I love you, too," he repeats, twining his hands in my hair as he angles my mouth even more.

He thrusts up against me, and I gasp against his mouth. "More."

He does it again, and I savor how sensitive I am, even with all of our clothes still on. My temperature rises, and I peel my shirt off between his hot kisses. His mouth is on the skin of my chest before I've untangled my arms.

"You're so beautiful," he breathes between the valley of my breasts.

Hands clutching my hips, he helps me ride his lap until both of us are gasping and sloppy.

"Should we move this to the back?" he says, reaching to unbuckle his seatbelt.

I hadn't even realized it was still on, but I shake my head. "Right here."

His eyes darken, narrowing on me as though I'm the only thing he wants.

And when he lets me stand to shimmy out of my shorts and underwear on the side of the road, mooning nature through the windshield, unbuckling his jeans and slipping them past his hips, he doesn't take his eyes off me. When I rip open a condom wrapper we miraculously found in the last store we visited with my teeth and slide it down his shaft, he blinks but keeps his wanting gaze on mine.

And when I crawl back over his lap, sinking down over his hard length, taking every inch of him until we are deliciously joined, he never looks away.

We move together, meeting each other's alternating thrusts and making up the difference when the other person is overcome by the pure headiness of this moment.

I think I know what it means to find myself.

It isn't linear, fitting into a neat little timeline. It isn't a puzzle you figure out and finish. And it isn't meant to discover alone.

It's the willingness to open yourself to the possibilities, to vulnerability, to love.

I don't know how I missed this before, but I can see myself in the reflection of Rhodes' eyes—the beauty and the shortcomings.

I see him.

I see me.

I see *us*.

39

RHODES

I wasn't sure what to expect when Paige told me about the farm we'd be staying at tonight.

I heard *farm* and thought cows, chickens, and horses. Lots of grass and trees.

Thirst Trapp Farms delivers on all of those things.

But there are also hot cowboys.

And yes, I feel secure enough in my newly developed relationship with Paige to say they are *hot*. Very sweaty and slick, too.

As we approach the old farmhouse with a slight lean, I roll down my window and note there are more than a few handfuls of wildflowers out front. "Hi, there."

The cowboy in low-slung Wranglers, a large belt buckle that could likely break a bone, and a hat he tips in greeting walks closer. "I'm Ronny. You staying in this for the night?"

"Yup." I sling my arm out the window, the last of the sun dialing back its warmth despite still lighting up the sky at nearly six p.m.

He tips his chin to where we pulled in. "You're welcome to stay in site two right back there at the end of the row of cabins, or you can stay in cabin two. We had a cancellation."

Paige leans across me, using my leg to rest her palm. I immediately come alive at the touch. "What does that cost?"

Ronny looks around to see if anyone might get on him about offering up a cabin, then shrugs. "Write us a review, and there will be no extra cost. We don't have someone coming until tomorrow, and as long as you follow the checkout instructions, I'm fine with it."

"And how do you feel about...cats?"

"In general, I like them, but if you're asking if you can have one in the cabin, well, then, let's just keep that between us." He tips his hat with a wink, and even I swoon a bit.

I look at Paige as her smile lifts, waiting for me to answer. "You want to stay?"

"Hell yeah, I do! I've been in a van for a week. I could use a real shower and a bed that isn't anywhere near a sink."

I whip back around to Ronny. "We'll take it."

"Great. You can park beside the porch." He starts to turn around, then pivots back. "My wife should be by in a bit. She'll make sure you've got everything you need."

We wave and park in front of the cabin.

"That guy looked..." Paige twirls her wrists, searching for the right words.

"Buff?" I fill in.

"No..."

"Like he should have his own sexy calendar?"

She purses her lips. "Not that..."

I snap my fingers. "Like all he needs is water to film a thirst trap?"

Her eyes widen as she turns in her seat. "You might be on to something there. I get where the *thirst* comes from."

We both laugh before switching to get-shit-done mode. "You can shove whatever you need in my bag. I can take Cleo inside, but we should probably keep her on the leash. There are a lot of animals here that could...you know."

"I know." She nods once. "Good plan."

Paige gathers a few clothes I plan to rip off her immediately as well as her toiletries and Cleo's food. With the backpack slung over my shoulder, I open the cabin door for us, gesturing with a dramatic wave.

She giggles and walks in first. The cabin is a mix of outdated floral printed furniture and finer finishes like the flooring and painted kitchen cabinets straight ahead. It's homey in a way that makes you feel you're returning to your parent's house after being gone for months.

"I'm going to check out the rooms," Paige says, moving down the hallway and out of sight.

I set Cleo down but keep her on the leash while she smells everything and jolts at every little noise. The throw pillows in the living room are perfectly situated with a karate chop crease in the center and lamps hovering over the couch and chairs.

"There are like...one...two...twenty condoms in this bathroom," Paige yells out to me.

I smile and thank the hot cowboy in my head. "Grab all of them." I'm about to sit down and stretch my legs out after the long drive when I hear Paige scream from the back room.

"Rhodes!"

But her scream isn't the only one I hear.

I'm already halfway down the hallway, bracing my hands on the doorframe right behind Paige, whose bag is dropped in front of her.

"What is it?"

She points at the form moving around in the bed before it pushes the covers off and sits up. "What the hell is all that screamin' about?"

Is that...an...

I flip on the light.

The older woman is now sitting on the edge of the bed, using her arm to shield the light from her eyes. The blackout curtains covering the windows were really doing their job.

"Um, hi," Paige starts. "I'm so sorry!"

"We were told this cabin was available," I add, hand sitting low on Paige's back.

The woman with curled white hair, a little askew from the pillow, a plaid shirt, and jeans with a few smudges looks at us through a squint. "It is available."

I peer around the room, looking for her luggage but come up short. "But you're here."

"I'm only here for a nap."

A knock sounds on the front door.

I lock eyes with Paige, then shrug to jog out and answer it. Swinging the door open, I find a much younger woman with cropped dark hair and a black cowboy hat that looks a lot like the one Ronny was wearing when we pulled in.

I feel like I should be wearing one now, too.

"Hi, I'm Tilly," she says with a smile and...stilettos? "Sorry for knocking so hard, I just didn't know if you heard me."

"Hi," I say. "Sorry about that. We were—"

The older woman comes trudging down the hallway, Paige on her heels.

"Granny?" Tilly's eyes narrow. "What are you—" She stops and pins the older woman with a glare that makes even me want to flinch. "You're sleeping in here again."

No question. She definitely was.

"I was checking to make sure the bed had sheets." Granny shrugs. "It does, so I'll just be going now."

Granny starts walking out when Tilly holds up a staying hand. "Not so fast."

My gaze slides between the two women, landing on Tilly, who says, "Are you napping in here again, Gran?"

"What?" Granny's tone is aghast. "I would never."

"You did just last week, too," Tilly spits back.

Granny props her hands on her hips now, mirroring Tilly's posture, and it looks like they're both about to face off.

I glance at Paige, trying not to move my neck too much in case I'll somehow get in between this face-off. Paige widens her eyes and does a few head nudges toward the sofa where Cleocatra has jumped up to strut across like it's a freaking fashion show. I dropped her leash in my haste to make it to Paige, and, deeming it safe, she went back to exploring.

All of our eyes slide to the curious Calico.

"Is that cat on a leash?" Granny asks, blinking a few times and rubbing her eyes.

"Uh," Paige gives me a panicked look. "Yes, it is. She's very well-behaved, though. And the guy out front with the hat and *very* snug jeans said it was okay."

Tilly breaks character but only for a minute to say, "His jeans are pretty great."

"I've never seen such a thing." Granny shakes her head at Cleo, then starts to laugh until it's a full-blown, leaning-over-with-her-hand-covering-her-mouth-while-the-other-slaps-her-leg-in-hysterics kind. "Cats don't belong on leashes," she squeaks out. "They belong outside by the barn catching mice."

"Granny," Tilly warns. "Don't you go tryna change the subject now. Why were you napping in the cabin again when Wyatt and Avery keep up a perfectly good room inside the farmhouse for you?"

Granny sobers as Paige goes to snatch Cleo. "Well, if you must know..."

Tilly sighs and crosses her arms. "I must."

The older woman, with a very slight limp to her gait, walks to the kitchen and opens one of the cabinets beside the refrigerator. All of our rapt attention on her, she pulls out a tin of what I believe are—

"Cookies," Granny says. "Wyatt and Avery don't keep these in the house, but I know you stock them in the cabins. Had a few too many this afternoon, and I got a little sleepy. Nothing to lose your head over, see."

Tilly rubs her forehead. "I'll buy you the damn cookies if that'll keep you from napping in the cabins."

I'm not sure if this is commonplace behavior between the two of them, but they seem comfortable enough with one another.

"It won't," Granny confirms. "But it's a start."

Tilly shoots another warning glare at Granny, but the older woman doesn't appear ruffled whatsoever. "They're Tempurpedic, Tilly! You can't beat that." She starts walking toward the front door, passing an exasperated Tilly before whipping around. "And one more thing...you're out of milk." She holds her hands up like she knows she's guilty but doesn't give anyone an opportunity to tell her that. "Don't forget to hug a cow while you're here!"

I peer over at Paige again, who is already looking my way.

"Sorry about that," Tilly remarks with a clap. "Welcome to Thirst Trapp Farms. Granny and her late husband built this place from the studs up, so we allow her a few luxuries here and there. Mostly involving cookies." She smiles, but it's forced. "If you want to enjoy the outdoor tub, it's just off the back patio and completely private. It's connected to a hot water hose on the side of the house. Feel free to wander around the property or ask Ronny or Wyatt to give you a tour in the side-by-side. And as Granny said, there is cow hugging, tractor rides, trail rides, massages, goat yoga, and new this year, a shooting range. All sign-ups are done through our website. There's also dinner tonight with the family in the farmhouse at seven if you'd like. Do you have any questions?"

I slide my hands in my pockets, amazed at the whole of this place. "I think we're good for now. Thanks again."

She smiles for real this time and gives a little wave before stepping back out on the front porch, pulling the door shut behind her.

Just kidding.

She pushes it back open. "Oh, and I'll bring you some new sheets."

With the door finally closed, I stalk over to Paige who's cradling Cleo to her, and pull at her waist. She rests her forehead on my chest and starts to laugh. "I never want to leave."

"I understand the appeal," I say against her hair. "Seems like they aren't short on entertainment around here."

She lifts her head and meets my eyes. "I was looking forward to using the bed, but I think we'll have to wait a little longer."

"There's always the outdoor tub."

She sets Cleo on the ground, removing her leash. "And you think your long legs will fit in there?"

"You won't take up much space," I say with a wink.

She swats at me, but I snatch her hand mid-swing as she says, "I'm not *that* short."

I smile down at her, then pull her flush against me. "No, you're not. You're perfect."

40

PAIGE

With new sheets on the bed and a very content Cleo, Rhodes and I walk hand-in-hand toward the farmhouse. After the show earlier with Granny, we couldn't refuse dinner. The promise of more entertainment was within reach, and I couldn't deny a home-cooked meal.

Rhodes takes the few porch steps two at a time, knocking briskly on the front porch screen door. "Do you think we should have brought something?"

I scrape my shoes on the doormat and scrunch my nose. "What, like the one hot dog we had left and part of a chocolate bar from the gas station?"

"I guess we're kind of running low," he says. "We should stop in town tomorrow before heading out. Ronny mentioned there were a few places to find all the essentials."

"You mean the cinnamon rolls the size of your head?" I cross my arms.

A smile lifts his cheeks. "Obviously we'd need to grab a couple of those, too."

"Obviously—"

The door swings open before I can say anything more, and a beautiful blonde woman with bright blue eyes and tanned skin welcomes us with a smile.

"You must be Paige and Rhodes." She's beaming, and I think I am, too.

"That's us." My eyes drift down to her shirt. Not because I'm a creep, but because Bob Ross is riding a leaping horse with rainbow beams around them both. The words *Thirst Trapp Farms* are scrawled above his head in an arch.

I need one of these shirts before I leave.

"I'm Avery." She opens the door wide to let us in.

I stop short, forcing Rhodes to ram into my back since there's a giant moose head with beady eyes, giant antlers, and a long snout that could probably fit my entire head.

"Oh, don't worry," she says. "That's Moosifer. He is one hundred percent dead."

I swallow. "Good to know."

Rhodes leans close to my ear when Avery starts down the hallway. "I'd say ninety percent dead. The shit he's seen will live on in those eyes."

I snicker as we toe off our shoes and follow Avery into a formal dining area set in its own room between the kitchen and living spaces. Wallpaper lines the walls as it did in the hallway with dark wood accents and family photos from just about every generation.

You can tell which were the more recent since Ronny and the owner, Wyatt, aren't wearing shirts in most of them, ranging from eight years old to...muscles.

"You're still here," Granny says with a big smile.

I match her expression. "Still here."

Avery pulls out a chair next to Wyatt at the head of the long oak table, and Ronny and Tilly sit on the other side from Granny.

"Sit by me," Granny directs us, then points across from her. "They bite."

Ronny rolls his eyes. "Sit wherever you'd like. We don't have anyone else joining us tonight."

I take the seat opposite Avery while Rhodes sits by Granny. I shoot him an apologetic look across the table. "Who else usually joins?"

Wyatt leans into the table. "All of the guests are invited, plus my parents, sister, brother-in-law, and their two kids. It started as family only, but like Granny always says, there's really no better time to get to know the Trapp family than at a dinner table."

"I don't say that," she retorts with a furrowed brow.

"I'm sure you've said it once," he says under his breath. "Ronny, would ya?"

Everyone bows their heads, and Rhodes and I quickly do the same.

"Bless this food, the people who are with us tonight, and those who aren't—"

"Don't forget Bob," Granny adds. "He's got a difficult heifer to deal with."

"And for Bob and his heifer," Ronny says before ending the prayer.

Avery sticks a spoon into what looks to be a chicken and potato casserole. "Which heifer is giving Bob some trouble?"

"The one who lives with him."

Everyone stills, and Wyatt asks: "You mean his wife?"

"Sure do," Granny confirms.

Avery curls her lips in, trying to conceal a laugh, but unfortunately, I can't help myself. I hide my grin and try coughing to disguise my chuckle behind my hand while Avery offers to dish everyone else up.

"You two married?" Granny asks, digging into her food.

I choke on my water, rendering me unable to answer. Rhodes takes this one. "No, just..." He stops himself, his fork hovering in the air to take his first bite.

I clear my throat and set my glass down. "We're dating."

Tilly smiles at me while chewing. "Good for you both."

"It's still pretty new," I confirm, fiddling with my cloth napkin until it resembles a rose like one does when nervous. I have my stint working at a restaurant to thank for this random skill. "Like yesterday."

Wyatt's eyes widen. "Holy shit—"

"Language!" Granny shouts before he can finish.

"Sorry, Gran."

Rhodes finds his voice. "We've been friends for a long time, though. Took me a while to figure out how to tell her."

"So he joined this blind dating experiment I was testing out with two other guys and told me his name was Roger, and then he eventually told me it was him when I had chosen Roger, so I bought my camper van and left the state."

Is there some kind of truth serum in this food?

Everyone stares quietly.

Nope. Just me.

"Do you all not talk where you're from?" Granny asks. "And what the hell is that?"

I stare at the rose napkin I'm twisting in my hands. "Oh. It's a rose. I learned how to do this when I worked at a steakhouse. They didn't have the best reputation around town, so I mostly spent my time making napkin art. And we do—talk, that is—I was just hurt and needed some space."

"I lied to her." Rhodes toys with the food on his plate. "And it was good we had some space to figure out what we both wanted. I picked up pickleball while she was gone and found I really loved it."

"What the hell is pickleball?" Granny's brows appear to be in a constant furrow.

"Gran!" Wyatt scolds.

She waves him off. "Rules don't apply once you reach eighty. It's like a free pass to say what you want."

Wyatt and Ronny share a look. Something tells me this isn't the first time she's likely made up her own rules.

Rhodes explains. "Pickleball is a paddle sport that combines elements of tennis, badminton, and table tennis. It's become rather popular recently."

Granny scoffs. "Or you could just go sling a few hay bales, shoot at some cans, hammer something to be useful in your distraction."

He shrugs, then finds my leg under the table with his.

"What do you both do for work?" Ronny asks through a mouthful.

Rhodes answers first. "I create stop motion videos with Legos and post them on the internet."

"That's really cool," Avery touts, then proceeds to ask where she can find them.

"I think I've seen them," Granny replies and Wyatt shoots her a questioning look. "What? I know my way around the internet now. Don't go acting all surprised."

Ronny's attention slides to me, and I realize it's my turn to answer.

Naturally, I have nothing to say on this topic because I don't have a job.

I have a van.

I have a cat.

I have a little bit of savings.

And a very cluttered resume.

"I...uh..." I can't even force myself to lie. "I'm in between jobs right now."

Rhodes smiles and nods in support.

I wish it were enough.

"Is that code for *you got fired*?" Granny's elbows are on the table like two stakes in the ground.

"Gran!" Tilly snaps, but I don't miss the laugh behind it.

"You were all thinking it."

There really is no filtering this woman.

I shake my head. "No, I, uh...I quit. I've worked a lot of odd jobs, and I'm just trying to find something I can make a career of."

"Almost anything can be a career these days," Wyatt says under his breath. All gazes slide to him, and he peers up. "I didn't mean that in a bad way. I just meant that's what happened to me, too. I moved back from San Francisco after being in a soul-sucking industry and started this business here to help out the farm. We worked hard to get this place going and made sure to include activities that would draw in visitors." His gaze meets Avery's. "But we did it. Now it feels like I get to do the best job in the world with my friends and family. We get to meet people from all over, work with our hands...it's a good deal."

I smile at him, forcing the tears pulling at my bottom lids to stay back. Everyone else seems to stumble upon their *thing*. The job they're good at or the thing they're most passionate about. But even after this road trip, I'm not sure what that is for me.

"You seem to know a bit about a lot of things," Wyatt says, directing his attention to the folded rose napkin I still haven't put to practical use on my lap like everyone else. "Maybe you see that as a difficult thing, but really, it's your superpower. You just have to figure out how to use it. I mean, I'd give you a job."

I'm sure he says this as a joke, but there's a moment where everyone is eating, absorbing the words Wyatt just said while I push the food around on my plate. I think he might be right, I just don't know how quite yet.

Tilly slowly pushes to a stand. "I—*we*—have an announcement."

Ronny wipes his mouth and then holds his wife's hand, staring up at her with so much love in his eyes.

"You bought more cookies?" Granny guesses.

Tilly exhales. "No, I—"

"You had to put a horse down?"

"I don't think that's a dinner table kind of announcement—" Ronny tries to say.

Granny snaps her fingers. "Pregnant!"

Everyone looks at Ronny and Tilly, waiting for them to confirm and save us from this awkward silence. I swallow and see Rhodes sitting statue-still out of my periphery. Did Granny really just guess their news?

Tilly's shoulders drop. "No, Granny, we're not pregnant. Now, would you just listen?"

"Damn it," Granny says under her breath. "I thought I had that one."

Tilly stands straighter again. "We're getting a puppy!"

Wyatt and Avery offer up congratulations while Granny mumbles something about her guess being better while Rhodes and I smile on. I wouldn't call it a fake smile on my face. I'm happy for them, really. Getting a pet is a magical experience I hope to repeat again soon. But I'm still held up on where I feel most stuck. One question still agitates my gut: what the hell do I want to do with my life?

41

Paige

"Are you still awake?" I whisper to Rhodes from beside him in bed. We came back after dinner and barely made it out of our clothes and into pajamas before falling into bed with exhaustion. It's still so crazy to me that he's lying on a pillow beside mine. Maybe that's why I can't sleep...

"Mhm," he mumbles.

He wasn't awake.

But I can't stop thinking about the dinner and need to talk to someone. Cleo abandoned her place by my head for the small chair in the corner of the room. I hope it isn't because Rhodes is in the bed with me now and solely based on the shag blanket draped over it.

"Do you remember what Wyatt said?" I ask him, staring at the ceiling with my hands clasped over my stomach. "What do you think my skills are?"

The sheets rustle as he turns to face me, sliding a hand over my stomach. "You're funny, brilliant, beautiful..."

"I mean actual skills," I say. "Ones that can help me pay the electricity bill and buy a loaf of bread and milk at the same time if I want."

"Wild woman," he coos. "Bread *and* milk?" I start to push his hand off me, but he holds it in place. "Okay, okay, I'll stop. Just let me hold you."

Instead of just his hand, he scoots his entire body closer to me, tugging my hip until my side is flush against him.

"I thought you didn't like to snuggle," I state, recalling our time in the experiment when he mentioned that.

"I never said that," he retorts. "I said I like to cuddle, but I also like my space. Plus, it's different. I'm not just cuddling anyone. It's you. You're like my...fated bond or my mate. Something like that."

The way he says this is revolutionary to my brain and makes my heart come awake like it's had twelve shots of coffee. I turn to face him and kiss the mouth that just said this to me. My hands wander up his chest, lightly pushing at his shoulder to pin him to the mattress so I can straddle him.

Instead, he grabs my wrist before I can sling my leg over him. "As much as I want this, as I'm sure you can tell with my instant hard-on, I'm not going to let you."

The dark room make it hard to see anything, let alone his expression, as I look down at what I believe is his face. "What do you mean?"

"I mean, I'm not going to let you use sex to distract you from how you're really feeling." He stretches behind him to the bedside table and pulls the hanging chain for the lamp, casting the entire room in too much light. He adjusts his pillow, keeping a hand on my hip. "Now tell me again, what's really bothering you?"

I sigh and face him, tucking a hand between my face and the pillow. "I went on this whole journey, had experiences that left me feeling empowered and *good,* but I still don't know what I'm going to do about my career. Where am I supposed to start? What do I do? What do I *want* to do?"

He listens, waiting for me to continue.

"I'm glad we're finally together; that isn't the issue. I just wish I had figured this part out a little more. The trip is almost over and..."

When I pause, he whispers: "Tell me."

"And I still have The Itch. It's not as intense, but it's there."

"The Itch?" he questions.

I suppose I haven't told him about it.

I take a breath. "The Itch is this sudden and intense need inside me for change. I can't describe it better than this, but basically, when I start to feel it, I want to upend something. I want to change jobs, get a new haircut, or travel in a van to Yellowstone."

"You've done all of those things in a matter of weeks," he points out.

"Yes, exactly! And The Itch just keeps reminding me I still don't have a plan for what's next. I know you said we'd figure it out, but what if I can't? I don't want to start a new relationship only for you to have to support me."

"I would, though," he says, eyes earnestly seeking something in mine. "I would support you financially, emotionally, physically, mentally...whatever you need, Paige. If you need more time to think about what you want to do, take it. Move in with me and think about it for however long you need."

"Move in?"

A smirk plays on his mouth. "I was going to wait until we got home to mention it, but yeah, I want to live with you. I want to see and be with you every day. I always have."

Tears spring to my eyes, but I don't swipe them away because they're evidence of just how much he makes me feel. How much he makes me want him. "Rhodes," I whisper.

"If you don't want to leave your parent's house, I'll move in with you—them."

A tear streaks down my cheek, but he doesn't swipe it away either, he just tracks it with his eyes as it absorbs into my pillow. "You'd do that?"

He exhales, eyes closing momentarily. "Of course, I would. God, Paige, there really isn't much I wouldn't do for you."

I know this because I've witnessed it for years. Rhodes has always been a constant in my life, there for me when I need or when I'm frantically entering another relationship because it's what I convinced myself I needed to feel settled. It didn't help, but Rhodes does. He's this anchor that isn't stifling but still holds me steady. It feels more freeing to be with him than apart.

He really believes in me.

And it makes me want to believe in myself.

"Would you live in the van with me?" I ask. Maybe it's a test, or maybe it's because it has been a thought that's crossed my mind.

His answer is immediate. "Yes. But we'd need a bigger bed."

I laugh and wipe at my wet cheeks. "Vincent VanGo doesn't exactly have the longest bed for all of your legs."

His voice deepens. "It's not just for my legs."

The hair on the back of my neck rises. "Oh?"

"It's to lay you out in every possible way," he says. "I love and respect you, Paige, but that doesn't mean I'm always a saint."

I bite my lip and use my foot to stroke up his calf. His breath hitches as I bend my knee and loop it over his thigh, getting closer until our noses are touching. The hand he had on my hip is now flattened against my back.

"I would live in a van for you," he whispers. "I would run a marathon—"

"You love running," I cut in.

"Okay, maybe that doesn't work then." He smirks. "I'd let you redecorate my entire apartment."

"That's better," I say with a laugh.

He presses us closer as if this were possible. "I would have run to Yellowstone to find you. I would go anywhere, see anyone, and dress in any themed Halloween costume you wanted."

I stroke the course stubble along his jaw, sinking my hand into his hair and loving the way he closes his eyes at my touch as if it's so good for him. "Despicable Me?"

"I'll be Gru."

"I make a better minion anyway," I say with a laugh.

He laughs, too, then locks eyes with me. "Take the pressure off yourself from always feeling like you have to have things figured out. You don't have to know where you're jumping next. That's one of the best parts about you, Paige. You aren't static in your passions. You have many and can fit in lots of different types of roles. But there's no rush."

I nod, then lean in to kiss him. But this time, I let our mouths explore, spark with love that turns into lust and takes over my senses in the best way as our tongues tease one another. His hands gently move me to my back and find new tracks along my skin that scatter my willpower.

That is, until I remember something. "My journal!" I push out of his arms in a rush, not even giving him a chance to get a good grip on me before sliding out of his embrace and bouncing around the room. "Where is it?"

He groans. "Tomorrow? Can we find it then?"

Not spying what I need after spinning in circles a few times, I slip my feet into my shoes and rush down the hallway to the front door, grabbing my keys for Vincent. He's parked right outside, so it only takes a moment to unlock the door to get the journal that Rhodes gave me. I'm back inside in what I believe is less than a minute if I were being timed, my heavy footfall pounding on the floors as I make my way back to the room.

I hold it up like it's a fish I just caught.

Rhodes is on his back, arms braced behind his head. "Your journal?"

I nod and crawl across the bed toward him. Sitting on my heels with the journal firmly gripped in both hands, I stare between the words I wrote to him and *him*. "For this entire trip, which really has only been a little over a week, I've written every word in this journal. For you and me. The random things I thought of, the weird mind trails, and the things I didn't know my heart needed to say. I wrote them all for you." I extend the journal with both hands toward him. "And as promised, I want you to read them."

He pulls his hands from behind his head, grabbing the journal with both hands in reverence. "The thing I didn't tell you was that I wrote letters to you, too."

My brows pull down as he reaches under the comforter and pulls out a journal to hand to me. It's leatherbound, like mine, with a ribbon holding its place somewhere in the middle of the book. "You wrote this much in a week?"

He exhales and pushes to his elbow. "I needed something to distract my mind when I wasn't playing pickleball. Instead of calling or telling you everything, I wrote it down."

I sink off my heels to sit beside him in bed, opening to the first page and running a hand over the inscription at the top:

Dear Paige.

42

Rhodes

Dear Paige,

I've tried and failed to figure out why you went on this trip.

It's hard not to think it's because of me. Of what I said…the kiss…the feelings. But I think I'm starting to get it, even if I don't have a lot of words to understand everything quite yet.

This journey for you is almost like the first test in our new relationship. Can we make it? Will I stick around? Will I take this opportunity to grow, too?

The answer is yes.

In fact, it's never been a louder YES than it is now.

We can make it.

I'm not going anywhere.

And you're not the only one who needs to work on themselves.

So, whatever comes, regardless of what happens, my answer is yes for you and me.

Always,

Rhodes

43

RHODES

Dear Paige,
    Life looks the same today.

Gym. Work. Pickleball.

But I feel like we have a shot at beating Jim and Agnes. I really do. And it feels good to have this kind of anticipation and hope in my life again.

Long live pickleball.

Oh, and I started seeing a therapist. It's weird to tell someone else my thoughts, but it also feels like the most natural thing I could do. Maybe that means I was ready. Yeah, let's go with that.

Always,
Rhodes

44

RHODES

Dear Paige,

Don't tell Amber, but I think she's getting worse at pickleball. I'm not sure how she's doing it...

Always,
Rhodes

45

Rhodes

Dear Paige,

I've been practicing being honest with how I feel.

I talked to Mom on the phone today and told her what was going on and how I felt. Mostly because, if anyone is going to keep me accountable in this journey, it's her. We saw my dad through a tough time, but we each had our own journeys. She wasn't all that surprised when I told her how much I love you. She said she's always known, which made me feel even more ridiculous for thinking I was somehow hiding it.

Instead of lying about how I feel about you this time, I'm writing it out. I want to give you the space you need, but I don't want to pretend that my feelings don't exist. Because they do, they're real and true and sometimes feel so big, they don't fit inside my body.

I love you, Paige.

I always have.

And I'm not sure why I thought that was so scary to admit. I convinced myself it would be the worst possible thing to be honest about, but it's not. It's kind of the best. My heart feels like it's contracting again, and I don't want to go back. I don't want to act like I can manage without the full breath this kind of love requires.

I like breathing, and I really like loving you.

Always,
Rhodes

46

RHODES

Dear Paige,

I need you to distract me from you.

Yes, I know that sounds weird, but you just sent me *the* photo—the one seared into my brain for all eternity—and I'm trying not to do anything about it.

Not because I don't want to!

No, because I want to so badly that I will wait. I want inside your head *and* your heart first. Then, I'm going to lick my way around your body until you're gasping, or I am. Probably both of us.

But not tonight. Not yet.

Always,
Rhodes

47

Rhodes

I can see why Granny would want to take a nap in this bed. It's delicious in how the mattress forms around your body. Not too soft, not concrete-hard.

Just right.

I stretch my arms above my head, open an eye, and peer to the side to find Paige not quite as I left her the night before. It would be rather uncomfortable to sleep with her legs over my shoulders and her hands gripping handfuls of my hair, but I wouldn't complain. Not a peep.

This morning, she's upright, leaning against the headboard with her knees pulled up and flipping through pages. At least this is what I can see through my squint.

"Paige?"

She hums in response but stays focused on whatever she's looking at.

The alarm clock on my bedside table says it's five a.m. This isn't a surprise to me since my alarm goes off nearly every morning at this time. My body is clearly used to waking without much prodding. I don't have set work hours, but I like to make it to the gym early before the after-school drop-off rush happens.

But seeing Paige awake at this time is odd.

The woman rarely sees what the sky looks like before eight.

Turning on the bedside lamp, I squint even harder when I look at her. "You're awake."

"I never went to sleep."

That explains that. "Why not? Did you have a nightmare? Upset stomach?"

Paige loves her sleep and has never had a problem knocking out, even after a three-shot espresso at five in the evening. Me? I probably wouldn't sleep for a week.

She stretches out her legs under the comforter. My journal is propped upright and open on her lap as she taps the top of a pen to her chin. "I was reading."

"Reading my journal?"

She lets the back of the journal fall to her thighs. "Well, yeah. I had a lot to catch up on—therapy, polo shirts, Jim and Agnes. And I was curious."

I sober a little, blinking rapidly as I angle my head to get a better look at her face. "But it isn't that long."

"You have more entries than mine does."

She's got me there, but it's only because I wrote every thought down. That journal was my companion. I wrote in it every time I thought about texting her, which happened to be a lot. But it became something of a release for me. It felt good putting my thoughts to paper, and even better when I realized it was helping me process.

She drops the pen in the open spine. "I reread it a few times."

Okay...

"And I made notes, or responses, rather. See." She turns my journal around to show me her meandering words, circling my entries as she flips through the pages. "I hope you don't mind. I just..."

Pushing to sit, I lean back against the headboard and peer down at my journal when she hands it to me. Every page has notes with her responses to every part of this week I put on the page.

Now that she's read them, I feel…lighter. The therapy of writing down my thoughts and feelings was made whole just by knowing my words were acknowledged somehow. I don't need to know what she said in response, just that she did.

I run my thumb over the blue ink from her pen. "I love you, Paige."

She pulls the journal from my hands slowly, then straddles my lap, cupping my face in her hands. "You said that a few times in your journal, too."

"I did," I confirm, tracing circles around her hip bones.

She presses her forehead to mine. "I love you so much, I can't even stand it. I almost woke you up at two, three, and four a.m. to tell you. But it's not like this is a huge revelation; just too good to keep inside."

I smile at this, letting my thumbs massage the skin under the hem of her pajama shorts.

"Maybe it's because we were friends before, we had a foundation or something like that, but once I realized—once I *let* myself love you—I couldn't stop it. It hit hard and so fast," she says, bowing over my chest to reach my lips and tenderly kissing me.

I run my hands up her ribs. "I know what you mean."

She kisses me softly at first, then harder, tilting my head up even more to deepen it. My head is spinning as I think about the years I spent hiding. I held my love inside, and it ate away at me. It was meant for more than me, and I get that now.

"Is this how you've always felt?" she asks, rolling her hips over mine and making it nearly impossible to think straight.

I roll her to her back and tug her shorts down, shaking my head. "No, because my love had a direction—it's always been you—but it wasn't until you felt it too that it became a living thing. It makes it so much better." My last few words dim to a whisper.

Her eyes roll back when my fingers trace the sensitive bundle of nerves between her legs, and I can't help but kiss her exposed neck. I pepper kisses along her collarbone and lower until she grabs the sides of my face and traces my jaw, watching me as I continue to touch her.

There's a new light in her eyes I hadn't noticed until this moment. It's realization mixed with awareness and so much love. She's read my thoughts, my love for her on paper, and this time, she was ready for them. It makes her look different in the way a woman who is loved looks at a man who will never stop loving her.

Our lips find one another, pressing softly at first before sinking into the comfort of feeling, touching, and opening. Her body is new but familiar as I explore the soft skin below her belly button and lower. When her muscles contract, and she clenches around my fingers, her mouth is forced open as she pants through her orgasm. The way she roughly shoves my boxers down and easily rolls one of the many condoms over me with light fingers has me aching for something harder.

I sink into her body as she curls legs and arms around me, and I can't help but thank love for this. It held on through dark times and even darker moments. It wouldn't let me go, and when I stopped trying to control it, love showed me exactly what it was capable of doing.

Paige grabs my face in her hands again as I slowly pump into her lithe body, one hand on her low back to angle her hips up even more, the other bracing my weight over her. We move and breathe together, syncing our sounds of pleasure to the beat of our hearts.

She's settling into my bones, my heart, my life, my forever.

Epilogue

Paige

Dear Rhodes,

    I know I haven't written in this journal in a while—okay, six months. But a lot has happened since then, and I need to tell someone, but it can't be the real you because you already know all of it. *Most* of it.

So, I guess in my weird way, I just need to write everything down to be remembered for all eternity. And because you're currently at pickleball practice, and I'm bored.

First, thank you for temporarily moving to Thirst Trapp Farms for a month with Cleo and me almost immediately after the road trip last summer. And then the fall and winter it turned into. This job has been everything I hoped it would be.

I get to hug cows while also expanding the assorted activities available to guests and the local community. Snowshoeing around the property, towel origami classes, Sip and Sew lessons for beginner sewers, and my personal favorite...book club!

Second, thank you for humoring me with short trips in Vincent Van-Go. My favorite times are when we drive him to a remote part of the farm, throw him in park, and crawl up to the roof with a mattress pad and blankets to watch the many flickering stars in the sky. I still get excited about the shooting ones, wishing upon them like I believe in their magic. And maybe I do since I always wish for the same thing: love.

The magic is working.

The Itch hasn't bothered me in months, and I think it's because I know you aren't going anywhere.

Third, thank you again for entertaining my family when they visited last month. I know it wasn't easy when Mom and Dad wouldn't shut up about the first plane ride they'd taken in over a decade. Or when Constance renamed all of the animals to cuts of meat—Drumstick (a.k.a. Amelia Egghart) has truly never been the same since—but you handled it all like you usually do with a smile and easy demeanor that is hard not to love.

Fourth, I think we should continue doing Sexy Saturdays. That is all.

Fifth and lastly, I would like the record to state that I did not, in fact, eat your leftovers like you claimed I did. It was Cleo. And yes, I know what you're thinking: *how could a cat eat pad thai with her paws?*

Great question.

It's because it was actually me like you thought. But for good reason! You're just going to have to wait to find out why later tonight when you get home from your cute little work trip doing your cute little videos. I packaged it up with a pretty bow and promise I wiped any residual pee off the stick.

We didn't plan it this way. We actually didn't plan this at all. But here we are, adding to the love we have. The kind that only fades a smidge when you leave your wet towel on the ground but is still stronger than I ever thought possible.

I don't want to do this with anyone else but you.

Annnnnnnd now I'm crying.

Damn these hormones! I blame you and Sexy Saturdays.

Yours Forever,

Paige

Epilogue

Dear Paige

Dear Paige,

I lied. Again.

But this time, I swear I had a good reason this time.

When you asked me what was in my pocket the other night, and I told you it was my boner…yeah, it wasn't. It was a small black box I've been moving around our two-bedroom cabin for five months now, waiting for the right moment to show you.

The hard part is there have been too many good ones to choose from. So, I've decided to just leave it in the fruit bowl and see how long it takes you to find it.

It's been a week, though, and I'm starting to worry about your eyesight. I mean, it's *right there*.

Anyway, I'm going to ask you to marry me. So if you find this letter before the ring…go check the fruit bowl.

Oh, and I know you ate my pad thai. You really aren't very good at keeping secrets, but I still love you.

Always and Beyond,

Rhodes

Epilogue

Cleocatra

I have found my true destiny.

Living on a farm is nothing like house cats portray it as. Sure, there is shit everywhere, and there are plenty of disgusting ogres who grunt more than speak, but it is not as dreadful as they want you to believe.

I have more mice bowing to me than ever before.

Birds practically fall from the sky by bullet or natural selection.

Trees beg me to climb them.

And I have a cat door now. A *cat door*. Can you even believe it? Coming and going as I please. I never thought I would be this kind of feline, gallivanting around in grass, rolling in dirt, and napping on the porch swing with that old woman who might think I'm actually a dog since she commands me to fetch.

But who really cares because I live on a farm, life is good, and Dad is going to marry my human before she gives birth to her litter. It's about damn time since she's been in heat for months now.

I hope she doesn't expect me to foster her kittens.

I just simply don't have the time.

I'm busy.

Very, very busy.

THE END

Thank you so much for reading! If you enjoyed this story, please consider leaving a review on Amazon, Goodreads, and your social platforms. It helps indie authors so much and would mean everything to me!

I also love connecting with readers on Instagram and TikTok: @authorchristinahill.

Acknowledgements

But didn't I promise to make it up to you with that ending?

I hope you enjoyed the ride that was Paige and Rhodes. The slow burn, the fun, the quirky characters, and lovable Cleo. It brought me so much joy to write them and even more to know how much they were loved by readers.

This book was *mostly* a secret until the very end, so, SURPRISE!

Thank you to all of my wonderful early readers who helped me with both books back to back. Haley, Janna, Samantha, Aly, Paige, Ashlyn, and Becca. You all were such a huge help in crafting this story and continuing the Poor Rhodes saga.

Tracey Barski, my hypervigilant pair of eyes, you are always a dream to work with and catch so many things I somehow missed through one million read-throughs. I love our partnership!

To Melissa Doughty for her extra special attention to Miss Cleo on the cover of this book. It was one hundred percent your genius and deserved a description in the book because of it. Thank you for making these covers so stunning!

To my family, my husband, Samuel, and our Fab Four crew, thank you for the "my mom wrote a book" shoutouts and endless "we're so proud of you" encouragements!

And thank you, my lovely readers, who have seen me through another book and are still here reading, reviewing, sharing, and laughing along with me. I appreciate you so very much.

All my love,
Christina

About the Author

Christina is a lover of love who has been writing stories in her head since middle school. She also holds the titles of "mom" and "babe" and lives in Montana with her four children, husband, and two cats she's obsessed with. When Christina isn't reading or writing, she is wrangling her kiddos, homeschooling, taking baths, baking, or raising a glass into the wee hours with her book club ladies.

For more information or to sign up for my newsletter, visit www.authorchristinahill.com

www.ingramcontent.com/pod-product-compliance
Lightning Source LLC
LaVergne TN
LVHW091717070526
838199LV00050B/2429